LUNA CHOSEN

LUNA RISING SERIES
BOOK FIVE

SARA SNOW

CHAPTER ONE
RUBY

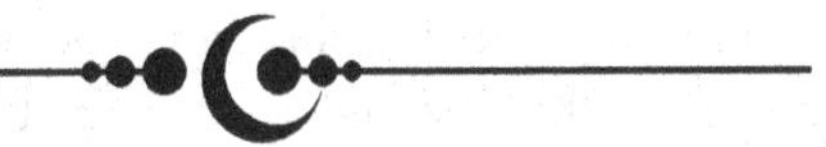

Not too long ago, I began my new life as a college student. But that was the beginning of the end of normalcy for me. Now, those college days seemed like a lifetime ago. Before then, I was a normal girl, an orphan. I was nobody. The only thing unique about me was the red hair that hung down to my ass.

At this moment, however, I was staring at Malcolm, my father and a black magic user, as he told me I'd been given divinity by a goddess—whatever the fuck that meant. On either side of me stood my two werewolf mates, Xavier and Axel, who looked just as confused as I did.

Thrust abruptly into the supernatural world after I saw Xavier transform when he saved me from being raped, it felt like I'd been continuously taking blow after blow ever since then. I had questions stacked upon questions with barely any answers.

I blinked rapidly. "I'm sorry, what? What do you mean I was given divinity?" I suddenly eyed the snake wrapped around Malcolm's neck, its fangs buried into his skin. My eye twitched. "Why is that thing biting you?"

Malcolm turned his head somewhat to look at the snake. "The deal I made with him was that he could feed on my emotions, and in return, he lends me his power."

The snake removed its fangs and then vanished into a smoke cloud, the same way it had appeared.

I couldn't imagine living like that, tying myself to a demon for power.

"As for you having divinity, I mean exactly that," Malcolm stated. "I'm only guessing this from the memory we just saw of your mother. What she said about your blood being that of the Goddess and never to spill it. It's a damn good guess, however, because it explains so much. The Goddess..." He glanced at Xavier and Axel. "...Your goddess saved Ruby at birth. She gave Ruby her powers, her divinity."

I rubbed at my temples.

"That can't be possible. A god just decided to give a mortal their divine power? Why?" Axel wondered aloud as his eyes drifted to me. "How?" he asked before turning Malcolm's way once more.

Malcolm shook his head, a frown on his face. "I don't know." He pinched his chin as he turned away. "But it would explain why Ruby has the power to kill vampires so easily. Now, we know why she has no ties to any other supernatural creatures," he added. His eyes narrowed as he looked me up and down as if he were trying to see the power lying within me. "You have power none of us has ever seen. If you learn to control these powers, Ruby, you'll be... you'll be able to do what you did to those vampires to any supernatural."

"Okay, no, I don't want to do that... to anyone." I held my hand up and took a step back. "This is more than I signed up for. As a matter of fact, I didn't sign up for any of this."

"Aren't you curious, Ruby?" Malcolm prodded. "Why would a goddess give you divinity? Why not a pureblood werewolf? Why save you?"

Malcolm appeared more excited than I did, and for the life of me, I couldn't understand why. He was getting so worked up, I was surprised his little snake demon didn't return to siphon off some of his extra emotion. I don't think he intended for it to sound as if I wasn't worth being saved, but that was all I could think of when I heard his comment. I said nothing as I walked away. I closed my eyes for a moment and could see my mother staring at me. The memory Malcolm had just helped me to see wasn't only a memory. I could feel it in my bones.

My mom had really been there. She had appeared to me as a ghost when I was a teen, but she had indeed been there in the mind link between Malcolm and me.

"I want to go back," I whispered under my breath as I opened my eyes. I turned around to tell Malcolm this.

He snapped his fingers. "Lovette; you were saved because of her. In the vision we saw of her giving birth to you, she asked someone to save you, not her. She wasn't talking to one of the nurses or a doctor. She was talking to the Goddess herself."

"So, are you saying the Goddess was going to save my mother, but she told the Goddess to save me instead?" I pondered.

Xavier combed his hand through his thick black hair as he sighed loudly. "This is insane," he muttered.

I agreed with him. "Who is this goddess, anyways?" I asked as I looked from one man to the next. "No one ever refers to her by name, and I've been too occupied to ask why. Since the Goddess is clearly real." I held my hand up. "Not that I doubted this, but if what Malcolm is saying it is true, who is she? What's her name?"

"She has no name," Axel explained, his hazel eyes twinkling for a moment as they reflected the light from above us.

"She's eternal and she's everything; she has no name," Xavier added, a certain reverence vibrating in his voice as he spoke, "She's just *The* Goddess."

I nodded and turned away. Looking down at my hands, I

quickly folded them into fists. I closed my eyes as I inhaled deeply, my powers buzzing under my skin. *So this is what I am?*

What am I? I was a human and an Enchanted, and I had a god's divinity, so what did that make me? It became obvious there was no name for what I was. There had never been another like me, and while many might have felt special in my shoes, I felt angry and confused.

A god would not give up their power for no reason, not without payment of some sort. What price would I have to pay for the privilege of living?

My heartbeat slowly started to increase the more my thoughts ricocheted off the walls in my mind. I heard footsteps come close and I pulled in the energy around me and released it.

Whomever it was stepped back, and I hung my head. I wasn't feeling happy my powers had just done what I wanted them to. Instead, I was angry that I'd just used the same powers I wanted to reject.

"Ruby?" Xavier called.

I shook my head, my back still turned.

"We don't know everything yet," he continued.

"That's what I'm tired of!" I snapped back as I spun around. "Every answer leads to more questions, and I'm sick of it. I've lived all this time without knowing who I am. If your goddess, the same goddess that caused me to be mated to the both of you, is the one that saved me, what is the cost, huh? Don't you see it? Everything, all of this has been planned. All of this."

Thinking about it only made me angrier. My life had been shit. Now, I'd discovered my mother, an Enchanted, put me in this position to begin with. I looked around the room. "If you're here, I fucking hate you."

"Ruby!" Malcolm yelled.

I turned to him. "Don't say my name! You don't get to say my name. You wanted to kill me, remember? No matter how you try to justify it, you wanted to kill me. So, honestly, *Malcolm*, you don't get to act like you give a shit!"

"Ruby, I get that you're confused right now and rightfully upset, but..." Axel's words trailed off.

I stared at him, my gut twisting further with anger.

His eyes flashed black at me. "Baby, listen to me."

My anger dissipated. Maybe it was the way he was looking at me or the endearment he had conveyed. Our relationship had only recently improved. Considering we started from a place where he hated the idea of me being his mate, affection coming from him was enough to soothe my swirling emotions.

His eyes returned to hazel.

I found Xavier looking at me with concern.

"I didn't stand a chance," I whispered, but I knew they could hear me clearly. "She knew all of this would happen to me." I shook my head at Malcolm.

As always, his face was a blank canvas, but his eyes glimmered with pity for me.

I went on, "Lovette knew from the start, from the moment the Goddess saved me, that this would be my life. She knew vampires still existed and would try to reclaim the earth." I shook my head. "My father wanted to kill me, and my mother was okay with me living the way I have, the way my life has been up until now. I don't know which is worse."

I didn't want to freak out, but I couldn't stop the rage coursing through me.

How much worse will this all get?

My body grew tense as I remembered the memory Malcolm and I had just seen of me when I was fifteen.

I rubbed a thumb against the scar on my wrist. The hardships of my life's hardships finally pushed me over the edge after Malcolm had approached me and told me he was my father. He had told me my mother died after giving birth to me, and I had just lost it.

That was when I first used my powers. When I burned a girl... that was it for me. I was already seen as a freak and outcast, so burning someone without even touching them just made things worse.

As the memory was revealed to Malcolm and me, my old feeling resurfaced—the utter defeat—the agony of my memory on replay in my mind.

I wished I'd never met my father.

I wished I hadn't known that I had killed my mother.

"It's starting to get hot in here," Malcolm observed, sounding a bit nervous.

"It's her," Axel murmured under his breath. "Ruby, maybe we should take a walk?"

"Let me be angry, dammit!" I shouted loudly.

The furniture around me was pushed away by an unseen force emitting from me. I wanted to be angry; I wanted to scream and cry. I wished I hadn't been saved. "Why does this all have to be so complicated? Huh?" The room's lights started to flicker as well, but I couldn't contain my powers, and I didn't want to. "Maybe the vampires won't destroy this earth. Maybe it'll be me—an out of control...thing!"

Xavier spun me around to face him. "That isn't going to happen. I don't know what exactly you saw, but with the powers you have, and maybe some you haven't even discovered yet, you're in a position to do more than Axel, Malcolm, and me combined. I'm not mad that the Goddess saved you. I'm not angry that you're my mate. I understand you feel used, but I—"

I shook my head and stepped back. "I can't..." I watched as the sadness in his eyes grew. I looked away, unable to bear it. Nevertheless, the pain within my own chest was growing rapidly, and I was not sure I could control it. "I need some space."

I walked out of the room, my hand covering my mouth to stop my sob as I walked briskly down the hall.

AXEL

I discovered Ruby in a well-furnished sitting room gazing thoughtfully at a life-sized painting of Lovette.

I found myself staring at the portrait alongside Ruby, mesmerized by the ethereal woman depicted there. "She was beautiful," I mumbled with admiration.

Ruby looked over her shoulder at me. "She was, yeah," she replied softly.

I took that as an opening that it was safe to join her. It was funny to think of me being wary of Ruby, but I now knew she could throw me across the room onto the bed with just a thought. I swallowed hard at the prospect and buried the images that appeared in my mind.

Once I was at her side, she held her hand out in front of her.

I stared at the scar on her wrist, the same one I first noticed a while ago. At the time, I had decided it was best not to ask.

"I thought I got this scar when I tried to kill myself when I was depressed," she explained. "I experienced depression after bouncing from foster home to foster home as a teenager, but it wasn't the precipitating factor for the suicide attempt." She swallowed hard, and her hand fell to her side as she looked up at the painting again. "Malcolm found me when I was fifteen. He told me who he was and who my mother was, and I lost it. The stress and pain from feeling responsible for my mother's death triggered my powers, and I hurt someone." She exhaled heavily and turned her back to her mother's portrait. "I went home and did this afterward. My mother appeared to me as I was dying."

I looked up at the portrait before looking at her once more. "She saved you?"

Ruby nodded. "She did, but she stole my memories as well. She placed the block in my mind." She turned to face me, tears in her eyes. "In the vision, while Malcolm and I were there, she was too... I don't know, but she was really there. She was there *in* the memory, with Malcolm and me. I don't know how to explain it, but she looked right at me."

"Maybe she was," I told her. "Lovette was powerful, very powerful. If she and the Goddess are responsible for all of this, she was more powerful than we ever knew."

Ruby sighed as she lowered her head and placed her palm on her forehead. "My head is killing me."

"Maybe you need to lie down," I suggested as I held her shoulders.

She stepped forward into my arms.

Surprised by this, I happily wrapped my arms around her and held her soft, warm body to mine. She felt so small in my arms, so vulnerable. "I hate seeing you like this," I whispered as I kissed the top of her head.

She gazed up at me. Her green eyes appeared brighter than they usually were. Without thinking about it too much, I dipped my head and kissed her passionately. She responded instantly, her lips meeting mine hungrily as her arms lifted to wrap around my neck. I snaked my arms tightly around her waist and lifted her off the ground somewhat.

All I wanted at this moment was for her to feel at peace, to feel some kind of happiness amid the mess that had become our lives.

She stiffened after a moment.

I placed her back onto the ground. Our lips parted. My eyes roamed over her face as I grew concerned at the cloudy look in her eyes. "Ruby?" I pinched her chin and tilted her head back.

She kept gazing blankly up at me as if she were seeing through me.

"Ruby?" I called again.

Her body started to shake.

The lights flickered above us.

I peered into the hall to see if it was happening there as well. I could hear Xavier and Malcolm rushing through the house to get to us with my heightened senses.

"Blood," she mumbled, her bottom lip quivering. "There's blood everywhere."

"Blood. What are you seeing, Ruby?" I urged her to tell me.

Her eyes rolled back, and she fell unconscious in my arms.

My heart skipped a beat as fear rushed through me.

CHAPTER TWO
RUBY

I saw a woman smiling up at a rather tall man. Her black hair hung in loose curls down her back. The man slid his hand around her waist and pulled her to him. I could tell he was a vampire from his pale skin—I could feel it in my bones. She held her head back, and he dipped his head to her throat. He looked my way, his eyes as red as blood.

Suddenly I stood amid a battle between werewolves, vampires, and humans, my heart hammering in my chest with fright. It didn't take long for me to realize it was a battle from long ago because of how everyone was dressed. Some were in armor wielding swords and wooden shields. The vampire Bleeders I got a glimpse of were pale, hideous creatures, wearing mostly torn, dirty pieces of clothing. Calling them 'rags' would be a generous description.

Even though I knew it was a vision, it felt all too real. I had to keep ducking and dodging to avoid the swords. I dove out of the way and fell onto my back as a werewolf pounced on me. He loomed above me, his giant claws poised to rip my body to shreds.

RUBY

It was the wind on my face that woke me, followed by the sound of singing birds.

I moved my arms and realized I was lying in the grass. I opened my eyes quickly, a headache throbbing at my temples. The twirling pale blue and white sky above caught my attention. It looked like paint being slowly stirred.

I sat up and looked around the never-ending garden as it stretched on further than my eyes could see.

"Where the hell is this?"

Before the vision, I was in Malcolm's home and talking to Axel, so why did I wake up in a garden?

"Axel?" I yelled as I got up off the ground, my eyes still taking in the garden, but I soon realized it was more of a meadow than a garden. "Xavier?" I called out again, but my voice just echoed around me.

There were countless kinds of flowers surrounding me, but the meadow was completely devoid of trees. I was utterly alone, and images from the vision I had before waking up in this place flashed in my mind. I closed my eyes and pressed my fingers into my tear duct.

So much blood, I had seen so much blood. *What the hell was that vision?*

The wind picked up around me, blowing the scent of the flowers up to my nostrils.

Is teleportation one of my gifts? I hope to God—or the Goddess— it's not.

"Malcolm!" I screamed. I figured if anyone could come and find me, it would be him. He'd been tracking me for years, keeping his eye on me, so wherever this place was, he'd better be able to find me.

I turned in a circle and froze as I spotted a large white tree I hadn't noticed before. I narrowed my eyes as I stared at it; even its trunk looked paperwhite.

"Maybe this isn't real," I whispered to myself as I started walking towards the tree. The tree looked as if it had been painted white—leaves, branches, trunk, and all—resulting in a stunning visual effect that literally took my breath away.

Standing alone in the meadow among the countless colorful blooms, and with such a peculiar look, the white tree's sight mesmerized me. As I drew closer, a white paw appeared from behind the tree, and an alabaster wolf stepped out from behind it.

I stopped moving, my heart skipping a beat as the massive animal, as large as a werewolf, pinned me with her gaze. She bared her teeth and growled low.

Fuck!

The wolf held her head up and began sniffing the air before sitting down, her eyes still on me.

Though she had stopped growling, I remained motionless where I stood. I wasn't sure if movements would spook her, and I had no intention of becoming dinner.

Long ago, Mathieu had told me white werewolves were a myth and that only the very first werewolf was white. Did that mean the wolf in front of me was the first wolf? Did this have something to do with the Goddess?

After a few minutes, the wolf got up, ruffled her tail, and turned around.

I watched with confusion, my heart hammering against my chest as the massive beast walked back behind the tree. I started looking around me once more, my need to get away from this place growing.

"Ruby?" a voice called my name.

I spun around to see a woman emerge from the opposite side from where the wolf had walked. My breath hitched in my throat as I looked right at my mother.

Lovette stared at me, a loving smile slowly grew on her lips.

"You're so much more beautiful in person," she said as she stepped closer to me. She held her arms out to me for me to come forward.

As much as my body wanted to run into her arms, I remained still. My features hardened as I stared at her. "You didn't have to take my memories."

Her smile fell away, immediately replaced by a saddened expression. Her white hair appeared to be as white as the dress she wore and the tree at her back. She looked angelic, and even though her luminous smile had dimmed, she was still so beautiful.

Since I had my father's red hair, I was trying to see what features besides her green emerald eyes I had. I could find none.

Is this woman really my mother?

"I didn't have a choice, Ruby," she explained as she moved forward.

I stepped back.

She sighed and moved her hair behind her left ear. "You might not believe me, but it was for your own good."

"My own good," I repeated. "Everyone seems to know what's good for me. That includes my father, who wanted to kill me *for my own good.*"

She looked away, her green eyes darting back and forth as the wind began blowing the flowers around us. "Your father went down a dark path."

"Because he loved you," I stated almost instantaneously.

The wounded look on her face hurt me more than I had expected. "I mean, he did what he thought was right to be able to find you. He was willing to do anything to get you back."

"As would Axel and Xavier," Lovette added with a knowing smile.

I started blushing. "Right," I drawled as I looked away. "Where is this? Where are we?"

Lovette stepped forward again.

This time, I didn't move away. The way she lowered and tilted her head to the side made me smile internally because I finally found something similar between us. I did that a lot.

"That's not important right now," she told me as she stopped in front of me. "What's important is that the block I placed on your mind and powers is now completely gone. Your memories will all come back over time, but your powers... those will be coming a lot faster." She lifted a hand, but it fell quickly back to her side.

My body had gone stiff the moment she'd moved her hand. I thought she intended to touch me. I tried my best to hold myself together, considering I was talking to my *'dead'* mother.

She explained, "I didn't only block your memories, but your powers too. Ruby, if I hadn't done that, your already-difficult life would have been far worse. I made it so your powers would start to be awakened once you met Xavier and Axel. Then you would have people around you who would be able to help you, supernaturals who would accept you, and not humans that would fear you, try to kill you, or try to study you."

"Why me?" I asked after taking a deep breath. "Why did it have to be me? Why did the Goddess give me her power?"

Lovette turned and walked away for a few steps, her palms open and brushed against a few tall flowers that stood high enough for her to touch without bending. Her shoulders rose and fell slowly as she inhaled deeply.

Where my red hair was almost to my bottom, hers fell past hers. "Only someone like you can bridge the decades of separation between werewolves and humans. You're the only one who will be strong enough to do what's needed in the end," she stated with conviction.

I shook my head. She was wrong about that. The Council actively wanted me dead, and even in the pack I was to be Luna for, I was liked by very few and trusted by even fewer. How would I possibly unite werewolves and humans? "You're wrong. I can't possibly unite werewolves and humans, and you know it.

Werewolves fear me right now, and the Council wants me dead. The only people they trust even less than me are humans and vampires. What did you mean when you said I'm the only one who will be strong enough? What will I have to do in the end?"

"You saw it before you came here," she said as she pointed at me. "You saw a battle between the species, didn't you? The vampires are succeeding in this invasion because the creatures of the world are more divided than ever. Ruby, you're special. You have the blood of a god running through your veins, a power that you can control instead of it overwhelming and killing you. That's what I meant."

I pressed a finger to the crease between my brows. The headache from earlier had stopped the moment I saw Lovette, but now it was coming back.

Lovette continued. "You could be mated to Xavier and Axel because you've never been *only* human from the start. You have Enchanted blood, but the divinity inside you overpowers that gene. That's why Natalie wasn't able to detect your Enchanted gene while testing you."

"But aren't Enchanteds descendants of the Goddess anyways? Don't all Enchanteds have the Goddess's divinity?"

She shook her head. "No. A long time ago, Enchanteds had more of her power, but it's become diluted over the years. She *gave* you her divinity. Her pure power was passed onto you, so it's much different from what you were already born with."

"Oh," I drawled. "What will I have to do in the end, then?" I doubted I'd be able to speak to her after this, so I wanted to know everything.

She merely looked at me without answering, an apologetic expression on her face.

I arched a brow questioningly, showing her that I was waiting for her response.

Still, she said nothing.

I rolled my eyes before looking away from her to stare at the tree. What was the significance of that thing, anyway? I glanced back at her.

She was still watching me. "How are things between you and the boys... Axel, especially?"

Was she serious? Were we going to have a cute mother-daughter chat about the two men my life had been intertwined with? "I, um..." I started to say but trailed off. I cleared my throat. My eyes still cast to the flowers below my feet. "It's going as expected. Xavier has been supportive of me and us from the start. Axel, not so much." I looked up at her.

She moved closer as she nodded.

I got the feeling she already knew how things were going with Axel and me, like everything else, but she wanted to change the subject. While I did want to know what was going to happen to me, it was clear she didn't intend to tell me. Maybe she couldn't, for some reason. Even though I wanted to hate her for making a choice that had turned my life into a freakish supernatural movie, I just couldn't find it in me to be angry at her any longer. I was seeing and speaking to my mother, the woman who gave her life to save me. I figured I'd better take the chance to have a mother-daughter conversation with her while I had it. This could be the last time I'd ever get to talk with her for all I knew.

"I um, I love them both, but..." I swallowed hard. "I feel angry at myself sometimes for caring about Axel."

"Why?" she asked.

I shrugged. "In the beginning, things were rough between us. He hated the idea of being tied to a weak human, and I hated him for the way he treated me initially. He abducted me, and... I should still hate him, but I don't. I can't. A part of me will always be angry about it, and I feel like I'll always be a little angry at myself for falling for him after what he did. Yet, I can't help my feelings. I care about him. He's done so much to help me. He left his pack behind just to be by my side. He's proven himself, and we've been growing closer. I just…" I sighed. "I know our mate bond brings us together no matter what, but am I a fool to love him after what he did?"

"I can't give you the answer to that. The men in Axel's bloodline have always been strong but very stubborn. He had his own pain that he'd been carrying with him for years. If your father is any example, pain makes people do stupid things sometimes. I can't tell you to forgive him. You have to decide if he's worth forgiving. However, what I can tell you is that you need both Axel and Xavier by your side. A new era is coming, but you will need them by your side in the war to come before that."

"I don't want to be a part of a war!" I exclaimed, my voice growing louder.

She gave me a pitiful look. "No one, not you nor anyone else, gets a choice. Fight or die. Those are the available options. Accept who you are, Ruby, or everyone dies. *Everyone*." She came closer and placed her hand on my shoulder.

Whatever momentary anger I had been feeling towards her faded, and I caved. My eyes began to tear up as I reached out and touched her as well. My hand didn't pass through her like I thought it would.

A tear fell from her eye as she yanked me to her.

We squeezed each other so tight I thought I would break her and she'd break me. I tried to hold back my tears, but they came rolling down my cheeks anyway.

"I'm sorry, Ruby," she whispered to me. "I'm sorry I allowed all of this to happen to you, about taking your memories and leaving you in the dark for so long, but I saw what was coming. The Goddess showed me who you'd become—a greater woman than I ever was."

I placed my forehead on her shoulder while shaking my head, and she pulled away. "I won't be. I'm a mess."

She chuckled as she cupped my cheeks, her eyes roaming all over my face. "You don't know what I do, and no, I can't tell you.

Too much is at stake. Sometimes we have to let the future unfold as it was meant to."

I rolled my eyes.

She laughed again.

My heart tightened because her laugh sounded precisely like mine.

"You're strong; that's why the Goddess picked you," she imparted softly. "Now you just have to believe that you are." She placed her hands on my shoulders and squeezed. "Trust yourself and your powers. Stop fighting them. Stop fearing them."

"I don't want it," I answered firmly. "I don't want the Goddess's power."

She pouted somewhat as she placed a hand on my cheek. "It's too late for that." Her hand fell away from my cheek and she grew serious. "You need to find General Presley. You will need his help."

I frowned at the mention of the human general who wanted me to help him, to help the humans. "Um, why? After the way we left him out in the open like that, he's probably dead."

She shook her head. "He's not dead. Find him." She stepped away from me, her eyes tearing up again. "You will figure it out. Trust your powers." She reached a hand out to me but kept stepping away from me. "I love you."

When I moved to go after her, my legs were rooted where I stood.

I sat up with a gasp, my eyes wide as I looked around the room frantically. I placed a hand over my pounding heart and gripped my shirt. When I inhaled, I could still smell the flowers from that meadow. I could still smell my mother.

My hand flew to my mouth, tears escaping my eyes as I turned onto my stomach and pressed my face into the pillow behind my closed lids. I could still see her. I could still feel her warm hand on my cheek. I laid there, my face in the pillow, as I cried for her to come back.

CHAPTER THREE
XAVIER

The night just seemed so silent, not even the insects were calling to each other. Ever since the vampires attacked, it was as if the animals had all gone into hiding. Vampires were indiscriminate feeders. They targeted animals like cows, dogs, goats, and horses as well. All warm-blooded animals were fair game for vamps.

I crossed my arms over my chest and inhaled, smelling oncoming rain in the air. I could feel the cold wind on my skin, but it didn't bother me. Werewolves had higher temperatures than humans, so I remained outside to enjoy the quiet night's peacefulness. Nights or moments like this didn't come around often, especially not when you were constantly on the run.

Axel had gone looking for Ruby after she stormed out of the room, and I allowed him. She said she wanted space, so I'd given it to her, but we couldn't leave her to be alone. I no longer felt bothered by them getting closer to each other. He was her mate just like I was, and I knew the pull she had. Therefore, I expected Axel was experiencing the same. Many might call me crazy or call him crazy for being okay with this, but this was how things had to be.

Fate, the Goddess, or destiny had thrown us together and it was clear now—we were stronger together than apart.

I would never reject Ruby; the thought alone made me ache inside, and I knew Axel wouldn't either. He loved her, and so did I. Her happiness and safety were all that mattered, and I knew I spoke for him as well. Despite this, I had to admit, the way we were currently living wasn't how I saw my life turning out before Ruby came along.

I saw myself finding my Luna and becoming the Alpha for my pack. I never expected to share my Luna with anyone, let alone another Alpha. The Goddess must be responsible for whatever allowed Axel and me to co-exist respectfully. Werewolves (and Alphas in particular) aren't exactly known for being good at sharing anything, much less a mate.

I uncrossed my arms and buried my hands in my pockets as I stared at the pitch-black forest ahead of me. It was a good thing Axel had gone looking for Ruby. After he'd found her, she got a vision and fainted. She'd been out for six hours now and counting.

I couldn't help worrying about her. The more we went down this path of finding out who she was, the more I felt it was best we let sleeping dogs lie... for now, at least.

Her powers were growing. Now that we knew where her ability came from, I couldn't help but think the divinity inside her might eventually be too much for her to handle. She was under an immense amount of pressure. She'd been living all this time with an essential part of who she was locked away. I wished she hadn't learned the truth about what happened when she was born before she truly understood how to control her powers. The more she learned about herself now, the more unstable she became.

Honestly, learning something like that would mess me up too. I would also be enraged to find out that I was just a pawn in the Goddess's chess game. I frowned as a thought occurred to me... *I am a pawn, actually. I'm Ruby's mate, and that makes me as much of a pawn as she is; so is Axel, for that matter.*

I clenched my fists as I shook my head and looked up to the sky. "You're playing with lives," I muttered and hoped the Goddess could hear me.

Malcolm had checked on Ruby multiple times already since she'd been asleep to see if she was okay. She was fine, but somehow she refused to wake up. Nothing he'd tried so far had worked, and so he decided to leave her be. Whatever was happening to her, maybe it was best not to interrupt it. Unfortunately, this was a poor time for her to fall into a coma. Malcolm's warding around his home was durable but could still be breached. Vampires were actively pursuing us, along with the Werewolf Council. By now, maybe the humans were as well.

The light to the patio switched on and a cloud of black smoke appeared beside me.

I sighed as Malcolm appeared from within it.

"Where did you get this?" he asked curiously as he held up Axel's book.

I had forgotten Axel had taken the book with him. I stared at the thick writing on its cover, *The History of the Damned*, and shrugged. "It belongs to Axel. It has a lot of info on vampires and how to fight them."

"You say that so lightly. You don't know the importance of this book, do you?"

I shrugged again.

His green eyes narrowed at me. "I'm not from the supernatural world and I know what this book is, while you and Axel don't? This is the only book in existence known to contain complete and accurate information on the vampire species for your information. I'm shocked something so valuable is not in the werewolf Council's possession under lock and key. How did Axel's family manage to keep it hidden from them?" He opened the book while shaking his head. "Unbelievable."

"Listen, up until the vampires crawled out of whatever hole they were hiding in, we thought they were extinct or even a myth. I wasn't exactly puzzling over where the vampire information was. The fact that they were gone was good enough for me," I said indignantly. "As for how Axel's family kept the book out of the Council's hands, you'd have to direct that question to Axel himself." I didn't care that this man was Ruby's father. He had threatened to kill her. Even though he felt like that was the only way to *save her* from the same fate as her mother, I'd never trust him around her.

I'd never trust him, period.

"Besides, you're a black-magic user. I don't doubt you know many things you probably shouldn't," I replied with distaste.

Malcolm shook his head. "Well, thanks to being a black-magic user, I found something no one else would," he retorted as he skimmed through the book's pages.

"What are you talking about?"

He looked my way, his eyes turning black. He then peered back down at the book, waved his hand over it, and the pages started to flip on their own. "There is demon magic emanating from this book," he replied as he watched the pages turn until the book was open at its center.

I grew curious.

"No one other than a demon or a black-magic user would have been able to sense it." He held his hand over the book, and a black mist began to flow from his hand to cover the book's pages.

We both watched as the pages began to change.

I moved closer as the writing on the pages morphed into pictures.

Once the mist cleared, Malcolm and I sported the same shocked expression as we stared down at the book.

"I—what? What is this?" I asked rhetorically.

Malcolm said nothing. His eyes were still wide in shock while glued to the book. "As I said, this is the only book that has accurate intelligence on the vampires."

I shook my head. "In all the stories I've heard of vampires,

vampires and werewolves have been at it since the beginning of time. The two species hate each other, so what the hell does this mean?" I couldn't look away from the picture of a female werewolf and a male vampire holding hands. The picture captured so much that I could clearly see the love in their eyes. A vampire and a werewolf together didn't seem possible to me.

The woman on the left page wore a deep green dress with a large green emerald around her neck, the color matching her eyes. The man on the right page wore a loose-fitting white silk shirt, its first two buttons undone with his black hair cascading down his shoulders. His eyes were a striking blue against his pale skin. Below them on the rest of the page was a war being fought between vampires and werewolves, a complete divergence from the love depicted between the woman and man at the top of the page.

I tapped a finger on the page. "Since you know so much, do you know what this means? Why would a vampire and a werewolf be holding hands like this?"

He shook his head. "I don't know. I knew *of* the book. I didn't know what was inside it. How did Axel even get his hands on this?" He turned to me with a questioning look on his face, as if he was the owner of the book and had just discovered who had stolen it.

"It's been in his family for generations, I think. Why?"

He kept staring at me as if he was trying to judge if I was telling the truth. "Okay." He looked back down at the book and turned a few pages before returning to the center. "I'll have to go through it thoroughly. There might be more hidden pages."

Suddenly, Ruby's scent engulfed my senses. I turned around as she stepped onto the patio.

"Hey," she greeted me, an apologetic look in her eyes.

I held my hand out to her. She took it, and I pulled her to me then kissed the top of her head. "Hey, how are you feeling? You've been out for a few hours."

"I, um... I feel okay." She gave me a weak smile, her eyes

looking a bit swollen. She looked Malcolm's way and cocked her head towards the book in his hand.

"What was your vision about?" Malcolm queried.

Ruby eyed the book in his hand as she answered, "I, ah, I saw a vampire, a man, and I don't know, it looked like he was about to feed on a woman, but she looked willing." She rubbed at her eyes and sighed. "Then I saw this battle from many years ago. People had swords and shit. Vampires and werewolves were fighting. It was... horrible." She looked from Malcolm and then up to me. "I could almost smell the blood."

"A battle, huh?" Malcolm repeated.

I knew what he was getting at.

Ruby nodded at him and combed her hair back from her face as the wind blew it forward. "Yeah..." She bit down on her lip. "I saw Mom."

Malcolm closed the book in his hand slowly. "During the battle?"

"No. After the vision ended, I was... somewhere else. It was a meadow. I don't know where exactly. First I saw a white wolf, and then I saw *her*. I saw Lovette. She was truly there."

"How?" I asked.

She shrugged. "I don't know. She told me she was sorry for taking my memories and that we need to find General Presley."

Considering she had been out for hours, I doubted that was all they had talked about, but I understood her not wanting to go into details. She had been given an opportunity most people never received—a second chance to speak to someone they loved and lost.

I shifted my weight from one foot to the other. "Why do we need to find Presley?"

She shook her head. "I... she didn't say, exactly, but I think it's for us to work together with the humans."

"Are you talking about the humans I saved you guys from?" Malcolm asked as he glanced at Ruby and then me.

Ruby nodded. "Yes. He wanted my help to fight the vampires. Mom said this isn't the first time vampires have tried to take over, but this time, they are succeeding because the creatures of the world are divided. We have to work with humans to have a chance at defeating the vampires."

Malcolm gave me a look the moment Ruby had said this wasn't the first time vampires had tried to take over.

I knew he was having the same thought as I was, about the werewolf that had sacrificed herself to end the war. Sometimes, I think about what life was like for supernaturals back then, being able to live openly and not in hiding as we did now. What had that freedom felt like?

Once this was all over, I guessed the supernatural community at large would have to come forward. Many would try to remain in hiding, and those who'd already been outed, like werewolves, would be discriminated against. However, I had hope that I'd live long enough to see this world the way it should be, with everyone being allowed to live openly and peacefully on the earth they were born on.

Supernaturals deserved that.

"What were you two doing, anyway?" Ruby suddenly questioned.

Malcolm opened the book once more and showed her the pictures we had found. "This book was emanating demon magic. I picked up on it, and then found this..." He opened the book at its center to show her the picture there.

Ruby reached out a hand to touch the woman and man. She pulled her hand away quickly, as if the page had stung her.

Malcolm quickly closed the book. "What is it?" he asked her. "Did you feel something?"

"It's them," she whispered. "It's the woman and man from my vision."

AXEL

I stared down at the page Malcolm had found in my book. I wanted to know how a book coated in demon magic had been passed down in my family for generations.

Werewolves could sense demons, smell them, but we couldn't detect their magic if it had already been used.

"Where did you really get that book?" Malcolm asked suspiciously.

I looked up at him and closed the book. "I told you, it's been in my family for years."

"It's coated with demon magic. A demon wouldn't have done that for free. They do nothing for free," he rebutted.

"I don't know," I told him for the second time. "I don't know why demon magic was used to hide pages of this book, okay? Or how a werewolf got herself involved with a vampire centuries ago. It doesn't take a genius to realize they were a couple, and that's without Ruby's vision confirming it. All I know is this book..." I tapped it with a finger, "...has been in my family for a long time. If you want more answers, I suggest going back in time, Malcolm. That's not even what's important here. What is really curious is the man and woman in the picture." I tilted my head to look at Ruby. "Did you see anything else? Anything you feel might be important?"

She shook her head. "It all happened pretty quickly. Nothing else is standing out in my mind right now, but I'll give it some thought."

"I don't get it," I muttered, more to myself than the others. "In all the stories I've heard, vampires and werewolves have always hated each other."

"That's what I said," Xavier added. "I don't think we have time to focus on this right now. Okay, a werewolf and a vampire were together years ago. Things were different then. I doubt it has anything to do with the mess the world is in right now."

"You're probably right," Malcolm agreed. "I'll keep checking the book. If there are any more pages, I'll find them. Maybe I'll find something that can help us now."

I gave the book to him.

Malcolm nodded. "You three can go look for Presley. If he's alive, I doubt he'll want to see me after I killed his men. If I discover anything else, I know how to find you." He said nothing else as he walked from the room, his snake appearing on his shoulders out of a black mist.

I looked at Ruby and her eyes met mine. I could almost feel her lips on mine from the brief kiss we had shared earlier. "Are you okay?" I whispered to her.

She nodded. "I'm okay, yeah."

"So, you saw your mom, huh?"

She gave me a tight-lipped smile and nodded.

I knew what it felt like to see someone you thought you'd never see again until the day you died. After the love of my life, Lilith, died years ago, I changed. I became quiet, distant, broken. I yearned to see her face, to hear her voice. Finally, she appeared to me again one night, and I got a chance to say my final goodbye. After she vanished again, it felt like I was losing her a second time. I grieved all over again, and a small part of me wished I had never seen her again.

Xavier and Ruby started to talk about the white wolf she saw, but I was busy just watching her, imagining what I'd do if I lost her too. Losing Lilith had been hard, painful, and the worst part was since she was a witch and our relationship had been a secret, I hadn't been able to speak to anyone about what was happening.

I didn't want to speak to anyone, anyways. Talking about it had been much too difficult.

Ruby, however, what I felt for Ruby, the completion she'd brought to my life, without her I'd...

I killed my negative thoughts.

A human had killed Lilith, and finding out my mate was

human sent me spiraling, causing me to make decisions I'd hate myself for until the day I died. I had hurt Ruby, insulted her, I had locked her away in—

I clenched and unclenched my hands as my self-loathing grew to a crescendo. Her even speaking to me was a blessing I'd never take for granted. Even back then, as much as I had wanted to hate her, I couldn't, and I couldn't reject her. Lilith told me not to harden my heart, but it happened anyway, and I wasn't able to accept Ruby the way I should have when she came into my life. Lilith had told me to keep *The History of the Damned* safe. For a while, I kept it close, but there didn't seem to be a reason to keep doing it as the years passed. I *wanted* to forget about the damn book. It had become a reminder of Lilith.

"Sorry, what? I didn't hear that." I turned to Ruby as I realized she was calling my name.

She sat down, her long red hair hanging over her shoulders. "Presley... Mom said I should find him, but I have no idea how. Apparently, I just need to trust my powers and they will help me."

"Then I guess that's what you do need to do," I told her. "Decide where we need to start. Wherever you go, we'll follow."

She rolled her eyes. She looked from Xavier to me and then back before smiling.

It did feel good to see a genuine smile on her lips.

"Yeah, okay." Sighing, she got up and ran her hand down the front of her black blouse. "I guess we can start where we last saw him."

CHAPTER FOUR
RUBY

I impatiently waited as Axel came to a stop on the road where we left Presley. That night, Malcolm killed all Presley's men to get to us, and then I discovered Malcolm was my father. It was just one of many eventful nights since. I'd lost count of how many there had been.

I kept tapping my finger on my thigh, my nerves getting the better of me as I tried to figure out how the hell I would locate Presley. We hopped out of the car together, the mid-morning sun warming the earth. Traveling by day was the safer bet... to an extent, at least. While we could avoid the vampires during the day, we still had to watch out for the humans hunting werewolves.

"Do you guys have his scent?" I asked them both.

"No," Xavier mumbled back as his nostrils flared.

"Too much time has passed," Axel added.

I sighed.

The road looked completely bare. It was as if the multiple exploded cars from that night that left the road littered with glass and dead bodies had simply vanished into thin air, spirited away by a supernatural janitorial crew Perhaps vampires had gotten to the bodies, but why were all the wrecked cars gone too? I doubted vamps had use for those.

We all walked away from each other in separate directions, our eyes on the ground looking for any clues.

I sighed. "Well, this is a dead end."

"There might be something here." Xavier kept looking around us as if he'd seen something, but the place was empty.

Axel kicked at a rock, sending it rolling off the road and towards the tree line at the side of the road. "This place was cleaned. If I had to guess, I'd say humans did the cleaning. Vamps wouldn't have bothered. There's nothing left to find now." He turned, walking back to the car.

I narrowed my eyes at the spot the rock had been. I headed over to the spot while snapping my finger to get the guys' attention, my eyes glued to the ground. "I found something." I closed my eyes for a moment and tried to remember everything from that night. I then opened my eyes and began turning in a circle, visually reconstructing everything in my mind as it had been that night. "When Malcolm attacked Presley, this is where he fell." I pointed to the drop of dried blood on the ground.

Axel and Xavier drew closer.

Xavier bent down and scratched at the small red spot on the ground. "Yup." He stood up. "That's blood, but it could be anyone's, Ruby."

I looked up at him. "But what if it's his? Maybe I can... use this." I stared back down at the blood and got on my knees. Inhaling deeply, I placed my hands on my thighs and sat back on my heels. "Okay, Mom, let's see if I can do this."

"What are you going to do?" Xavier asked.

I honestly didn't know. "Not be afraid, like Mom said. I guess?" I shrugged, with no confidence at all that I even could do this. I exhaled and held a hand out to hover over the blood on the ground. I closed my eyes and shuffled forward a little. I waited and waited, but nothing happened. My shoulders slumped as I made a face. "So much happened just now," I mumbled sarcastically. "Trust my powers, my ass."

"Hey," Axel interjected. "You can't just wait for something to happen. Relax, open yourself up. Your power belongs to you. You don't belong to it. Stop waiting for it to do something, okay? Trusting yourself means opening up to whatever needs to happen."

"You know, you're not just as dumb as they say you are," I teased with a grin.

He smirked. "No one says that. Not unless they want to die," he whispered as he stood.

"Try again," Xavier urged.

I nodded, a little more confidence seeping into me.

I stared down at the blood for a moment. I breathed slow and even as I stretched my hand out again, and closed my eyes. I reached out to the power within me. As I did, that buzz of energy seemed to be there. Instead of waiting for it to act, I grabbed it and began telling it what to do.

The darkness behind my lids began to fade. An image appeared far away, gradually coming closer and becoming larger as it did. I rocked back as I was thrust into an image of the night we had left Presley.

Vampires had appeared shortly after we left. Since I'd met the vampires being referred to as Skins, the ones that looked human, I figured the creatures I was looking at were Bleeders, with their pale, hairless skin. They started feasting on the bodies on the ground when Presley woke up. He killed one of the vampires and was about to be attacked by another one when his backup arrived. Cars carrying more men appeared, killed the vampires, and collected the bodies on the side of the road. Presley was helped into the back of a vehicle while the wrecked cars were placed on truck transport.

Presley watched while six additional bodies were placed alongside the bodies of the men Malcolm had killed in the back of a van. The vampires had been killed, but those men lost their lives in the process of retrieving Presley. I could almost feel the anger and regret emanating from him.

A tall man—his brown eyes as dark as his skin—approached Presley. "What happened here?" he asked.

Presley didn't look away from the van with the dead bodies as he replied, "We retrieved the girl, but she was taken from us before we made it back to base."

The man continued to stare at Presley.

After a while, Presley finally looked at him. "Okay," he said with a nod. "We'll head back to base."

The vision cleared. I opened my eyes and got to my feet shakily. I rocked back on my heels to fall.

Xavier reached out and grabbed my arm.

"You okay?" Axel asked.

"What did you see?" Xavier added.

I released his arm after balancing myself. I tried to calm down, but I could still feel my power humming in my veins. I swallowed as I squeezed my eyes shut, then opened them.

Xavier frowned. "Your eyes are black."

"I know," I replied strenuously. "I-I'm trying to stay in control, but it's—not working. I, um, I saw what happened after we left Presley. Vampires found him, but so did his people. They headed back to their base, wherever that is. When we find that, we'll find Presley."

I walked around and away from them, my fingers pressed to my temples. The last thing I wanted to do was to hurt them. My powers had done what I had wanted. Now I had to learn how to come down from the high of using them. "We should head back to Malcolm's and figure out how to locate—" a hand wrapped around my elbow and yanked me to the side. I looked up at Axel in time to see a bullet pierce his shoulder.

Confused and in shock, I couldn't get the words out to ask what the hell was happening before Axel pulled me behind his back. I stared wide-eyed at Xavier.

His eyes had turned black as he hunched forward, his eyes on something behind us, and he growled while his fangs elongated. He fell to a knee and began to shift when a wolf appeared out of nowhere and sprang at him.

Axel released me and rammed his shoulder into the wolf, stopping it from attacking Xavier, who was still shifting.

I looked behind me to find a man with a scar under his left eye, his gun aimed at me. Everything was happening so quickly that when he pulled the trigger, I stood frozen.

Axel appeared in front of me and he shot hit him in the back. His hands resting on my shoulders dug into my skin, but I couldn't say or do anything as he began to lower to the ground. His hold on me tightened as he coughed up blood.

"Axel?" I softly said as I fell to the ground with him, my eyes wide and stinging with tears. "Axel!" I screamed as the fight between the unknown wolf and Xavier rang in my ears.

Shaking with my chest hurting as if a hand was wrapped around my heart, I looked up to see that three more men joined the first that had shot Axel.

They were all dressed in full black, along with another transformed wolf— then it hit me. These had to be the men from the Werewolf Council. They had to be.

I looked down at Axel on the ground, blood soaking through his shirt at the shoulder as his hand gripped at his chest.

I felt a rush of energy from within the earth rise and engulf me. As I stared down at Axel's black eyes and he peered into mine, black veins began to make their way up to his neck from the wound in his shoulder. Embers of my anger ignited into a roaring fire as my rage consumed me.

I got to my feet slowly, an electrifying sensation coursing through my body. I felt better than I ever had before. I could feel the power within me, filling me up completely. I felt invincible. I felt like I couldn't be touched.

I channeled my anger from Axel was now lying on the ground,

his skin turning pale, all because he took bullets intended for me. "You shot him," I accused through clenched teeth, my eyes on the man with the scar under his eyes.

He had just made the biggest mistake of his short life.

"I was aiming for you," he replied with a smirk.

I lost it. I stopped thinking of everything except my rage as my power erupted inside me like a volcano. All I could see was the man with the gun still in his hand.

The sickening smile on his face faded as his hand holding the gun began to rise.

The men around him backed away nervously.

"What the hell are you doing?" one of them shouted.

"What the hell, man? Lower the gun!" another added as they kept backing away.

"It's—it's—her," the man I was targeting choked out.

I forced him to throw the gun to the ground as I held my head up, my fists clenched at my sides.

He fell to the ground, his back arched as his clothes began to rip. His shoulder snapped and he howled in pain as his left leg followed. "Stop—her!" he yelled.

The other men looked my way.

I didn't care what they did. There was nothing they could do to stop me, and this man was going to pay for what he had just done to Axel. I could no longer hear Xavier and the other werewolf fighting. There was nothing except my rage and my power coursing through me.

The man's transformation continued, his bones breaking and rearranging as fur began to burst from his skin.

"Stop! Stop!" He cried out, his face now shifting as a snout began to appear where his nose and mouth were.

I flicked my wrist and his head snapped to the side, the sound of breaking bone echoing in my ear, but my rage didn't die as I had expected it to. If anything, it was fueled even further when the other men aimed their guns at me.

I held my hand out, warmth rolling from my core to the tips of my fingers.

One of the men dropped his gun. He flashed his fingers as the now-hot gun burned him. His eyes widened as he watched the weapon on the ground begin to melt.

Before the other men could do the same, their guns started to melt as well.

No one else would be shot today. "Axel won't die alone today." I held my other hand up, causing their bodies to go stiff until the first bone snapped in each of them as I controlled their change.

As I called on the wolf inside them to come forth, someone yelled my name. "Ruby! That's enough!"

My hands fell to my side, my palms still warm as I looked into Olcan's strange central heterochromatic eyes, the blue outer rim of his eyes fading into brown in the middle. I said nothing as he stepped past his men.

I narrowed my eyes at him.

He stopped, his arms held up in surrender. "I only want to talk." He lowered his hands, his eyes roaming my face and body.

I saw the excitement within his eyes, and it made me sick. First, he wanted to kill me, and now he was fascinated by me? I looked down at Axel, the veins now covering his left cheek. I pointed at him as I looked at Olcan.

His face twisted with confusion.

Then Axel groaned as if in pain, grimacing as he rolled to his side.

I opened my palm as the bullet that had been in his back flew into my hand. I stared down at the bullet in my palm and watched as it turned to dust.

"Heal him." I brushed my hands on my jeans. "Or everyone here that I don't care about... dies."

RUBY

While driving to Olcan's house with Axel lying in my lap in pain, I was distracted enough to get my powers under control. I had been trying not to panic at the black lines spreading across his face or the way his lips were getting darker while his skin got paler.

He looked like he was dying.

Now, at Olcan's house with the sick bastard himself sitting across from me, I wanted nothing more than to wring his neck with my own hands.

"So," Olcan drawled as he crossed one leg over the other. "You're Lovette's daughter, huh?"

"Yes. What do you want, Olcan? You wanted to talk, so talk," I countered.

He chuckled.

There had just been something about this man that had bothered me from the moment I met him. Maybe it was his odd eyes and bald head that created a bizarre combo for me. "Where is Axel?"

He uncrossed his legs and looked towards the door. "He's safe. He was shot with a bullet that's poisonous to werewolves, but he's being treated as we speak. He'll live."

"That's good news for us both," I remarked.

He smirked. "There is something different about you, Ms. Saunders. I wonder what it is. The impressive amount of power you have, maybe?"

"Is that what you want, Olcan? You always seem to want something from me. The last time we met, you wanted to kill me, so what do you want now?" I did not intend to waste time chit-chatting with this man.

The mischievous look he'd been wearing vanished and a serious expression took its place. He looked every bit of the no-nonsense Council member you'd expect him to be. "The first time we met, I didn't know about your significance, your power, or your lineage. You being Lovette's daughter changes a lot." He gestured to me.

I shook my head. "Drop the act, Olcan. You would have killed me anyway and buried the truth about me being Lovette's daughter. You would have done anything to hide the fact that Lovette had a child with a human." I spat the words at him.

The angered look in his eyes at the mention of Lovette being with a human brought me more satisfaction than I'd expected.

"You can help the werewolves," he declared after a moment of utter silence. He was changing the topic. "You have the power to fight with us, to protect us from the vampires and humans. You're one of us."

"I'm not one of you," I told him bluntly. "I'm mated to werewolves, but I'm half human and half Enchanted; that is what I am. I will fight for all creatures against the vampires, and that includes humans." I flicked a finger. "Humans shouldn't have attacked werewolves while vampires ran free as the real enemy, but they were scared and confused. Besides, no matter how powerful you think I am, I am not powerful enough to save werewolves from both human and vampire enemies at the same time. The vampires alone are barely being held at bay." I stood from my chair. "We need allies. I don't know about you, but I'd much rather make allies of the humans than the vampires. Humans and werewolves need to work together to defeat the vampires. It's the only way any of us stand a chance."

He laughed loudly at this before settling once he realized I wasn't joking.

"I'm not kidding, and you know it. You also know fighting the vampires alone will get us all killed. They outnumber us, and those numbers grow every night."

"An alliance? With humans?" His eyes rounded. "Listen, Ruby, you're new to this, new to this world. Something like that will not happen easily," he said condescendingly.

I opted to ignore him. "You're new to this world as well,

Olcan, or have you lived in a world overrun by vampires before?" I arched a brow questioningly.

He rolled his eyes at me.

I didn't care how he felt. I had a point to make, and I was making it. "You say an alliance can't happen, but the same was once said about a human being mated to a werewolf, right?"

"Okay, Ruby." He held his hand up. "Tell me, how did you find out you are Lovette's daughter?"

I clasped my hands behind my back as I answered, "The block in my mind was removed."

"And what else was revealed? How did you get these powers? It's because you're a hybrid, yes?"

I shrugged. "Does that even matter right now, Olcan? Listen, I'm going to be honest with you. You're asking questions that I refuse to answer right now because I frankly don't trust you. You could easily try to use any information I share with you against me. Since we both know you wanted to kill me, how about proving you are trustworthy before expecting me to share sensitive information with you? Help with the alliance between werewolves and humans, and I'll share what I learned about myself with you." No way would I spill everything to him. For all I knew, he was just waiting to know where my powers came from so he could kill me where I stood, or worse—and I did believe he was capable of worse.

"Fair enough, Ms. Saunders." He held his hand out to me.

I squinted as I peered down at it. That had been easier than I thought. "What's the catch?" I asked him.

Olcan shook his head. "No catch. You said you'll tell me all you know, and that's all I need. Do we have a deal or not?" He tilted his head to the side as he held his hand out.

"We have a deal." Still feeling suspicious, I shook it firmly before quickly pulling away.

CHAPTER FIVE
THE VAMPIRE GENERAL

The sound of humans screaming in pain and agony never got tiring.

The smell of fresh blood was abundant in the air as the Bleeders maimed and tortured the terrified humans they found hiding in the basement. The pitiful people were smart enough to avoid hiding in the upper rooms where we would've found them immediately. Yet their foolish plan merely delayed the inevitable, especially since there was only one way in or out of the basement.

It hadn't taken long for the Bleeders to sniff them out and find them, but I gave them an A for effort.

I had already sorted out the humans to be killed from the humans to be turned. Now all I had to do was wait for the Bleeders to feed before we could move on. I released the young woman in my arms, her body hitting the ground with a thud. The beautiful pale blue eyes that had drawn me to her were now pale and lifeless.

Running my tongue over my fangs, I swallowed the last of her blood.

One of my soldiers walked towards me. "General," he greeted me, his eyes briefly drifting to the blonde-haired beauty at my feet.

I could have turned her, but though she was beautiful, I found her high-pitched voice annoying. I certainly wasn't interested in listening to *that* for centuries to come.

"We've picked up on the girl's scent, though it is faint. They must have been out during the day. We do know she's traveling with wolves, and they are on the move."

This news piqued my interest. The wheels in my mind began to turn as I stared down at the girl at my feet.

The growls and hisses of two nearby Bleeders penetrated the air as they fought over what appeared to be a man's arm.

"Enough!" I yelled.

They both dropped the arm and held their heads down in shame as they backed away.

I knew the hunger inside them, their insatiable taste for blood. The difference between Bleeders like them and Skins like me was that I could control my thirst. "Find her location by tomorrow night," I commanded before looking at the man still standing by my side, his red eyes on me. I walked off towards the building's exit. "I'd like to meet Ms. Saunders in person."

I exited the building and stepped out into the night that had been my beginning and end for more years than I cared to count. I didn't remember what it was like being human. I couldn't even remember what the sun felt like on my skin.

Nevertheless, I could remember the very moment the Queen herself turned me and made me her son as if it was only yesterday.

We'd waited so long for this, to feel the cool night air on our skin again, to live openly and not cramped together like ants. Decades... it'd taken decades for us to get to where we were now. We'd waited for the right moment for so long, and I'd be damned if I let one little girl ruin it all.

———— ••• ————

RUBY

Maybe making a deal with Olcan hadn't been the wisest decision, but what other choice did I have? It felt like I was running out of time, like something loomed on the horizon and I wasn't prepared for it. The world was reverting to the Dark Ages, and I felt like the walls were closing in on all of us.

The power inside me—the Goddess's power—was strong; it was intoxicating and like nothing I'd ever felt before. Yet, it was also scary. I lost control when that man shot Axel. All I had wanted was to see him suffer.

I killed a man in cold blood. Each time I thought about it, a chill ran down my spine. Even worse, I felt nothing at all when I did it. Killing him—taking his life—hadn't fazed me at all. This was what Mom should have warned me about—the superiority and emptiness that came with having the power of a god. I had no idea how I had controlled his shift. I just looked within him to the animal at his core and called it forward without really thinking about it.

I think it made sense, though. The Goddess created werewolves, so no doubt she had control over them as well. I had her power, so I had that control as well.

"This is so fucked up," I whispered to myself as I walked down the quiet hall to Axel's room.

Olcan wanted to know everything I knew. He wanted to know where my power was from and what I was capable of. He'd seen what I could do, and I didn't want to even think about what would happen if he ever got the kind of power residing within me.

I hadn't been able to sleep last night after arriving here. Between worrying about Axel, finding Presley, and wondering if the Goddess had made me a monster, I couldn't fall asleep for even a minute. My thoughts kept repeating on an endless loop. Before I knew it, it was dawn and another day of living this hell.

For the entire day, I locked myself in a room to practice using my powers. What other chance would I get other than when I was in danger and had no choice but to react? If I did not learn to control my abilities, I feared I might be consumed by them.

I might have almost burned the building down once or twice, but in the end, I was able to control the heat within my body. Calming down wasn't as hard as it had been before. The first time I had killed vampires, my powers had backfired on me, burning me as well. It wasn't an experience I cared to repeat.

Lovette had said my powers would start to grow quickly, and I could see that happening.

"Xavier!" I called as I spotted him at the end of the hall. I hadn't seen him all day.

He held his hand out to me.

I drew closer and slid my hand into his.

He kissed the back of my hand before kissing my forehead, and the tension between us from when I had told him I needed space at Malcolm's dissipated.

"I heard you practicing today." He pulled back but kept holding my hand.

I nodded. "I was trying to."

"How was it?" He moved my hair behind my ear, his eyes darting back and forth over my face.

"Hard, but I'm getting there, I guess... I, um, I don't know who that person was that killed..."

"Hey, hey," he interjected as he pinched my chin. "You were protecting yourself and us. It was either them or us. Olcan's loss is on him. He attacked us."

I tried to find comfort in his words, but I could still hear the sound of the bones breaking in that man's neck as I had killed him. "Yeah," I drawled, "You're right. What have you been doing all day? I didn't see you even once."

"I went out for a bit. I've been working with Olcan's men to try and track down Presley's base." He released my hand to comb his hair back.

I noticed the bags under his eyes. *It looks like he didn't get much sleep, either.* "And?" I probed. "Any luck?"

He shook his head. "Not yet, but we're still working on it. We found one working computer in this dump, but as expected, there is no internet connection to check if there are any army bases close by. One could have been created after the invasion."

"Okay," I mumbled as I stepped to the side to lean against the door to Axel's room. "I hope Presley doesn't hate us now after what happened. He might have been the only human willing to work with us."

"Well, if his mind has changed about an alliance, we'll just have to change it back again," Xavier said with a casual shrug.

I hoped it'd be as easy as he was making it seem.

"I'm surprised Olcan agreed to the alliance," Xavier stated.

I didn't intend to tell Xavier, or Axel for that matter, about the deal I'd made with Olcan. They would object to it, of course. "I don't trust Olcan, but at least he sees that we can't win this war against the vampires by standing alone. Fighting together is vital for our survival."

"Yes, and I don't trust Olcan either. He's a snake. I doubt he'd try anything after seeing what you're capable of," he added. "He just can't be trusted. If he agreed to this, something must be in it for him, and it can't be good."

Xavier was right about that. Something was indeed in it for him.

"I heard the other wolves talking about you," he went on. "News about you being Lovette's daughter is spreading fast. Olcan would have killed you to keep it a secret, but now he can't touch you. The backlash would ruin him."

After Olcan saw what I was capable of, I was sure he wanted to cut me open and dissect me even more than he did before. I frowned. "They're talking about me?"

He nodded. "You're Lovette's daughter; you're royalty. Now

that you're clearly a major asset in winning back our world, don't be surprised if you start getting treated differently."

I said nothing. I wasn't sure what to expect, but I'd never been one to love the spotlight. I knew almost nothing about my mother other than she was loved and respected. Many looked up to her, and now they might look up to me. What if I let them all down? What if the Goddess picked the wrong girl? "Oh, okay," I whispered.

Xavier chuckled, no doubt noticing the terrified look on my face. "Relax, Ruby. All I'm saying is everyone else will now see what I've always seen—that you're special."

He leaned down and I closed my eyes as his soft lips pressed to mine in sublime union. He held my waist firmly and pulled me close to his hard body, and I reached up to wrap my arms around his neck. He broke our kiss to trail light, soft kisses down my neck, and my body shivered. It was so easy to get lost in the moment anytime this man touched me. "Breathe," he whispered in my ear.

I did as he commanded, inhaling deeply and exhaling through my mouth.

He held me tight. "Don't think about what anyone has to say about you or what they are expecting from you. Okay?"

I nodded. "Ok."

He placed a final kiss on my shoulder. "Has Natalie contacted you?"

I shook my head.

He looked away, his brows furrowed. "She hasn't mind-linked with me either. I'm worried about them. I don't know if the pack is safe or not." He ran his hand down his face, pulling his cheeks down. "Natalie should have contacted us by now."

"I'm sure they're okay," I told him with a smile. "But I can try doing a mind link myself. That should be easy compared to the things I've done so far. Right?"

He placed his hands on my shoulders. "You're getting stronger, but mind links aren't as easy as they seem. You could really hurt yourself and the person you try to make the connection with. Let's not push your powers too far."

I moaned at the feeling of his hands running up my shoulders and neck to cup my cheeks. I knew he was only worried about me, but I wanted to help. I had only started training myself during the day when I had gotten tired of sitting around, doing nothing. Axel was still out of commission, and Xavier was busy with Olcan. Sitting on the sidelines was driving me crazy.

For the most powerful person here, it seemed like I wasn't needed for shit unless there was killing to be done.

Becoming a weapon was not how I saw my life turning out. You didn't need a college degree for it, that was for sure. Not that I had a college to return to anyways. My scholarship was toast by now.

"I'm not pushing myself. In the beginning, I could only feel my power when I lost control and it was triggered. Now, I can constantly feel it buzzing just beneath my skin. Lovette said I should trust my powers, and I'm starting to. I can contact Natalie."

His hands fell away from my face. "I know you're getting stronger. I just want you to be careful, that's all. As you said, they're probably okay. If Dad wasn't okay, I'd feel it. Let's focus on one thing at a time. Right now, we need to focus on Presley."

I wanted to fight him on the matter, but I knew he was right. "Okay."

Smiling, he kissed my forehead and backed away. "I'm going to find Olcan. I hadn't asked him before, but he must know something about the vampire queen. Maybe I'll tell him about what Malcolm found."

"Okay," I murmured, wishing we didn't have to rely on Olcan of all people for help.

He turned away and left.

I watched him as he walked away. When I could no longer see his towering muscular figure, I groaned and palmed my face. After a moment, I turned and knocked on the door to Axel's room.

"Come in!" he greeted from the other side of the door. When I entered the room, Axel was sitting on the side of the bed. He looked up at me.

As I closed the door behind me, my eyes roamed over his shirtless body. The black veins had completely disappeared, and he looked much better since color had returned to his skin. "You heard Xavier and me talking, didn't you?" I asked as I sat down beside him and scooted further up on the bed, so my legs dangled just above the ground.

"I can't say I could help it," he replied with a smirk.

I bobbed my head. "Werewolf hearing, right?'

"Right," he answered with a grin.

I chuckled. "How are you feeling?"

He looked away, the smirk on his face slowly fading. "Better," he answered after a while.

I had a feeling this wasn't entirely true. I placed my hand on his that rested on his thigh. "You saved my life," I said softly.

He shook his head as he flipped his hand over to hold mine. His thumb caressed my hand. "You saved mine, actually," he whispered as he leaned over and kissed my temple.

Axel being affectionate always caught me off guard.

He squeezed my hand before releasing it and turning to face me. "How are *you* feeling?"

I gazed back at him in confusion. I wasn't the one who'd been shot. "Ah, I'm fine."

He kept staring at me expectantly.

I smiled. "I'm fine, really. I'm keeping it together."

"What you did was—"

"I know," I said sharply, cutting his words short. I knew what he wanted to say. "I know it was crazy, and no, I don't know how I did it. I just reacted. But even so, I still feel—horrible inside."

"He tried to kill us, Ruby. He doesn't deserve your sympathy. I'm sorry you had to do what you did. However, Olcan is responsible for that man losing his life. His approach for 'just wanting to talk' was foolish. Ruby, if anyone attacks you—be it werewolf, vampire, or human—I want you to defend yourself."

"Yeah, Xavier said the same thing about Olcan being responsible," I told him as I stared down at the glass of water on the bedside table.

"And he was right." His baritone voice vibrated with the strength of his conviction.

My eyes slid to his.

He reached out and picked up my hand. "Now, tell me where Olcan is, so I can rip his fucking heart out."

The fact that he said it so calmly and casually made me believe he truly intended to kill the man. "He agreed to the alliance with the humans. I'm sorry, but you can't kill him."

Axel released my hand and stood. "That just means I can't kill him *yet*."

With him being shirtless, I couldn't look away from his rippling abs. Shaking my head, I swung my legs onto the bed and laid down to get comfortable. Closing my eyes, I sighed as Axel's scent from the pillow engulfed me. "I wonder where Reika is right now. I'm surprised she's not here with him," I commented, my eyes still closed.

The bed dipped at my feet as Axel sat down. "Probably with the Enchanteds; it's every species for themselves right now."

"Sad world," I mumbled. The lack of sleep was finally catching up with me. "It feels like it's been a week since I last slept."

Axel picked up my legs and removed my shoes. "You need to rest, Ruby. You need to keep your strength up."

The door flew open, and I sat up quickly, my heart in my throat.

Axel was already on his feet, ready to defend.

One of Olcan's men stepped into the room. "Vampires were spotted a mile out, and they are approaching us quickly. Get ready. We're going to be attacked." He walked swiftly out of the room before either of us could respond.

Axel turned to look at me, his body suddenly tense.

I stared at him. "Are you well enough to…"

He nodded. "Yes. I can shift. How the hell did they find us so quickly?"

The stronger I grow, the stronger my scent becomes. "They must've followed my scent. We need to find Xavier and Olcan," I answered hastily as I headed for the door.

Axel grabbed his shirt before rushing out the door behind me.

As we dashed through the hall and down the stairs to find the others, my heartbeat started to pound in my chest. I didn't think I could ever get used to this life. I'd never get used to being hunted, and I'd never get used to all the near-death experiences.

What had changed, however, was my confidence. We might be the ones under attack, but I knew the vampires wouldn't be leaving this place alive.

Axel and I entered the room.

"We need to get Ruby out of here," one of Olcan's men announced.

"Forget it. I'm not going anywhere," I stated firmly.

All eyes turned to look my way.

"I don't need to run, and neither does anyone else." I called on my power, allowing its enticing hum to fill me. "If we stand together, these bloodsuckers won't stand a chance." I knew my eyes had just turned to black, and I grinned widely. "Let's show these asshats why they should be afraid of the Big Bad Wolves!"

"You heard the lady," Olcan announced, his voice echoing through the room as his multi-colored eyes turned to obsidian as well. "Let's remind these vampires who we are! We've hidden in fear long enough!"

CHAPTER SIX
RUBY

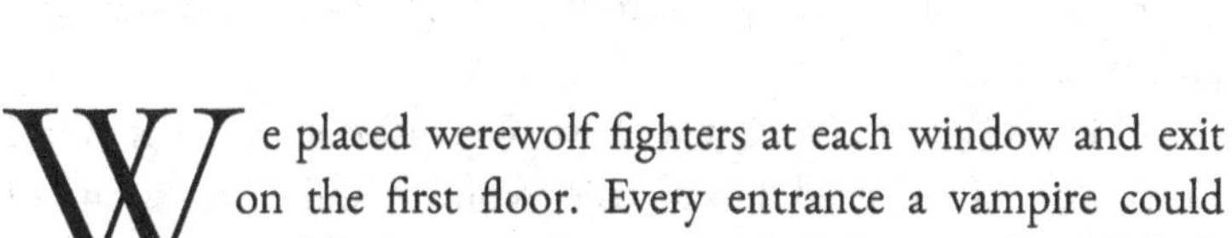

We placed werewolf fighters at each window and exit on the first floor. Every entrance a vampire could possibly enter was being guarded. Some wolves shifted, while others maintained their human form. We all waited impatiently for the impending battle.

Axel and Xavier stood on either side of me, while Olcan and one of his men chose to position themselves next to Xavier. Given Axel's current sentiment toward Olcan, this was probably a wise choice on his part.

While I heard nothing but silence, I knew with their heightened hearing, the werewolves could hear everything outside. Each time I started to speak, Xavier or Axel would hold their hand up to stop me... I needed to remain quiet. Vampires had heightened hearing just like werewolves, and the ones outside were no doubt listening for us.

We all had our backs to the wall beside the front door, the werewolves fangs and claws at the ready as I tried to hold onto the bravado I had felt earlier.

I hadn't caught a whiff of the rancid scent that followed vampires like fleas, so I guessed they weren't close enough to us yet.

Axel nodded at me.

I leaned forward and waved a hand to gain Olcan's attention. "Did you manage to find Presley?" I whispered as softly as possible, my lips barely moving, but I knew he could hear me clearly.

He shook his head. "Not exactly." He leaned forward and whispered back but loud enough for me to hear, "We did find car tracks, so the base can't be far from here. I'd say 15 miles, maybe, or perhaps more, since we weren't able to sniff them out while searching today. I sent two men ahead to see if they could locate the base, but they should have returned by now."

"We have to go," I whispered to Xavier.

Olcan shook his head vigorously. "Not now, when vampires are on our heels."

"I know, Olcan. I meant we have to go as soon as this is over. I just... I'm just worried about losing control and hurting one of you. I don't have control the way you might think I do."

"That doesn't matter, Ruby. In war, control isn't the most important thing. In war, we have to break ourselves free from the restrictions of doubt that could hold us back. We have to do what needs to be done because our opponents will do anything to win. Those Bleeders who are coming won't have control over their bloodlust. I hope you know that. They intend to kill us all, and we need to think the same. You need to focus on doing maximum damage to them in order to ensure we all make it out of here alive."

"Okay, I get..." my words trailed off as the vampire's scent clogged my nostrils.

The sound of breaking glass echoed through the house.

Axel and Xavier both placed their hands across my body as the sound of wolves in battle traveled to our ears.

"Get to the second floor!" Axel yelled.

I shoved his hand away from me. "I'm not running!"

Xavier grabbed me around my waist before the words had completely left my lips and threw me over his shoulder.

"Put me down!" I yelled. "You assholes!"

Xavier was already halfway up the stairs as he ignored my screams.

While upside down, I watched as the front door was kicked open and three vampires rushed inside, one being tackled by Axel.

Xavier and I got to the second floor just as a window to our left shattered. He lowered me to the ground quickly, and I had to catch my balance as a vampire barreled into him.

This was the first time I'd seen a Bleeder in person, and my skin felt itchy at the sight of the ghastly thing.

It looked hairless and pale with jagged, sharp, bloody teeth. Its wide red eyes were frantic and unfocused, while its animalistic growls and hisses were chilling.

Xavier slammed the creature into the wall and sliced its throat open with his claws. He then stuck his arm into the creature's chest and ripped its heart out.

We watched as its lifeless body fell. In my peripheral vision, I noticed a Bleeder rushing up at me from the stairs.

My powers reared inside me as I spun around to face it. I held a hand up as it dove at me, and the vampire froze, suspended in mid-air.

Its eyes were watching me as drool fell from its mouth.

"Burn, bitch," I said through clenched teeth.

Its skin began to bubble.

I released it, causing it to fall to the ground where it began to shriek and bend in all angles, its thin skin melting off its body. The smell was disgusting, but the angered hiss of another vampire down the stairs had me backing away.

The moment it lunged to charge up the stairs, a massive wolf tackled it to the floor. I turned and ran with Xavier behind me as two more vampires appeared. There were more of them than I had imagined. From the sounds of howls and growing banshee-like screams, I knew they were pouring into the house still.

Ringing pinged in my ear, and I spun around when I heard breaking bones.

Xavier was shifting, and the vampires were right behind him. They obviously weren't going to wait until he'd completely shifted to attack.

I held both hands out, squeezing my eyes shut as I dug deep into that pit of intoxicating power inside me. When I opened my eyes again, I could see the white energy around us and the black aura surrounding the vampires. I opened myself up to the energy as I stepped around Xavier, calling it forward as Xavier continued to shift behind me. As I released the buildup of energy pulsating through my body, a scream rolled up my chest to burst forth from my lips.

The vampires were knocked back, their bodies breaking from the force. They fell like broken dolls, their pained cries hurting my ears.

Xavier ran around me, his claws scratching against the floor as he charged towards the vampires. I watched as he ripped into them and smiled at their weak attempts to stop him. He grabbed the last one by its thin ankle and began dragging it away.

Shaking my arms from the tingling sensation within them, I moved back the way we had come, following Xavier and the vampire. I could still feel the earth's energy around me, almost begging for me to consume it, to use it.

I started running, my legs pumping hard when a window to my left shattered and something slammed me into the wall. My hand shot out, my intentions to send the vampire snapping its jaws at my neck flying back through the window, but it bit down on my arm and wrapped its arms around me.

We went falling through the window together, its revolting odor burning my eyes as we fell. I grabbed the creature's face as we fell and forced all the heat inside my body into my arms. I turned us so the vamp was on the bottom to take the brunt of the fall, but even so, the impact rattled me.

I rolled away from the hissing and shrieking creature, trying to ignore the sharp pains in my back and ankle.

Looking down, I realized my ankle was broken. I bared my teeth as it suddenly snapped back into place. I sat up to stare down at my feet in shock.

Okay, that's new.

Looking around me, I stood up and winced as I heard a crack in my back as if a bone had reset itself. I hadn't figured self-healing would be so painful. I'd seen the guys do it so many times without even flinching.

I looked down at my arm while the vampire's cry grew quieter and quieter, the bite on my hand starting to burn. I watched as my blood dripped onto the ground and loud hissing filled the night. The vampires were no doubt being drawn to me, but I didn't move. I didn't run. I didn't feel fear.

My face twisted with rage as they started to circle me, their red eyes like headlights in the night.

I kept turning in a circle, looking from one to the other before holding my bloody arm up. "Hungry?"

Some of them held their heads back, veins protruding from their necks as they inhaled deeply, while others bared their fangs at me.

"None of you deserve my pity," I whispered to myself. I exhaled as I let go of my emotions and inhaled as much energy from the earth as I could take.

One rushed at me and I slapped it across the face, sending it rolling on the ground.

Now realizing I wouldn't be easy prey, the others took a step back.

I could see their aura, the darkness surrounding them, and I tilted my head to the side thoughtfully.

I looked down at my bleeding hand and clenched my fist. As adrenaline coursed through my body, my heart pounded in my chest, and my breathing was labored. I looked up as one of the vampires rushed forward, and I just *reacted.*

The vamp came to an abrupt halt just in front of me, its clawed hand inches away from my face. I stepped closer until its face was inches away from mine. I envisioned all the corrupt energy inside the vampire flowing into me. When the corrupt energy obeyed and flowed into me like I wanted it to, it wasn't unexpected. Yet, the pain that came with it took me by complete surprise and left me breathless. Nevertheless, I gritted my teeth and kept going. After the first vampire lay dead at my feet, the intense energy draw became a like chain reaction, jumping to the next closest vampire.

One by one, they crumbled to the ground, their hands over their ears or clawing at their own chest as I took their lives. I started to tremble the more I took from them as I caught glimpses in my mind of grisly scenes of torture and horror that would've made crime scenes from serial killers look positively friendly.

Arms grabbed me around my waist and pulled me back from the vampires, and like the others, it fell to the ground.

I pulled away from the person holding me without even looking. I could taste blood on my tongue as I kept hearing the screams of so many dying humans.

I fell to the ground and began forcing the energy I had taken from the vampires into the earth. I couldn't hold it. I knew if I did, I'd die.

I fell back on my ass once all the evil was all expelled from my body, and I looked behind me.

Xavier stood there, naked. "Ruby?"

"I'm fine," I answered hoarsely as I got up.

I swayed as if to fall.

Xavier grabbed my arm quickly.

Although my eyes were blurry, I blinked rapidly at what looked like a man standing in the distance. My vision cleared, and I narrowed my eyes as I realized it was indeed a man.

His red eyes told me he was a vampire. With the semi-darkness around us, I could barely see his face, but his eyes were bright enough to be seen from the distance between us.

"We're being watched," I mumbled under my breath to Xavier.

He raised his head to look as well. He released my arm and stepped forward, a growl rumbling in his chest.

I was too busy finding it odd that I could almost feel fingers inside my mind. My face twisted with discomfort as I looked away from the man to hold my head.

Axel and Olcan appeared by our side, the sounds of battle inside the house now growing faint.

The moment Xavier rushed forward, no doubt to chase the man in the distance, Olcan grabbed him and pulled him back. "Don't!" he yelled.

Xavier yanked his arm for him to release him.

"That's a General, you idiot! Look at the uniform. Does that look like a Bleeder to you?" Olcan added.

We all looked in the direction of the man in the distance. I couldn't see his clothes, and I didn't care to. All I cared about was getting rid of the feeling like he was inside my head. *How is the bastard doing it?*

I created a block in my mind, a metal wall if you will, and the prying fingers started to slip away.

I frowned as the General turned around and headed away.

Axel stepped forward. "Why isn't he attacking us?"

"I don't know," Olcan replied in a hushed and confused voice. "But we should count ourselves lucky."

"If he's a General, shouldn't we try to capture him? He could lead us to the Queen!" Xavier exclaimed.

Axel nodded, sharing his frustration that the vampire was now gone.

"No matter how strong she is," Olcan began as he pointed at me, then frowned at my disheveled state, "Which doesn't look like much, right now, Ruby's not ready to fight a General. Generals are turned by the Queen herself. If we kill one, we'll lead the Queen right to us. That's a fight we can't win right now." He looked towards the forest. "However, if a General came here after she already lost one, she must really want Ruby."

"Well, he just walked away without even trying to take her," Axel pointed out.

"Maybe he wanted to see what she's capable of first," Olcan guessed with a shrug. "Or maybe it was a message that they can take you whenever they wish."

"I felt him inside my mind," I revealed.

Everyone stared at me in silence.

I shrugged. "It was as if he was trying to read or see into my mind."

Wiping blood from his hands, Olcan stepped around us to head back to the house. "You better hope he didn't actually see anything, because if he did and tells the Queen, whatever chance we had at winning was just lost."

* * *

OLCAN

We left at dawn after burying all the men I lost. Being raided by those vampires last night had ruined my plans. All I had to do now was help Ruby with finding this Presley person, and my part in this mess would be over.

Good men... I had lost good men.

I clenched my fists as, even now, her scent licked at my nostrils. When night fell, we'd be attacked again, no doubt. There was no hiding for her anymore, not while she smelled like a walking candy.

"When you guys escaped from Xavier's pack, you masked your scents somehow. Can't you do that now with Ruby?" I asked Xavier and Axel.

Ruby turned around to look at me. "It doesn't work on me anymore. We tried."

"Of course it doesn't," I mumbled to myself as they turned around to continue walking.

"Pick up the pace, Olcan. We need to find the base before sundown," Xavier urged impatiently over his shoulder.

Do these kids really think I'm a machine like they are?

Ruby stopped walking. "Can we rest for a little?"

Xavier nodded. "Okay, five minutes, but we really need to keep moving."

She sat down immediately with an exhausted sigh.

The road looked deserted, the forest on either side of us quiet except for the sound of a few birds and the wind in the trees.

I removed my bag and took a bottle of water out of it. Gulping it down, I watched Axel and Xavier chat among themselves.

I'd noticed Axel had changed. He wasn't the same brooding asshole he had been when I first met him. Xavier had changed as well. He didn't seem to be the naïve, immature kid he used to be. He seemed more like the Alpha he was born to be, ready to lead. The person that interested me the most, though, was Ruby herself.

It was laughable how those three thought they were successfully hiding where Ruby's power originally came from. I already knew she possessed divinity given to her by the Goddess. All I needed to know to successfully set my plans in motion was how she survived for so long with so much power.

Last night, she had killed those vampires by absorbing their life energy—their soul, one might say. It had almost killed her, but she had done it. I know this group didn't hold a lot of love for me; few people did if I was honest. I didn't care what anyone thought of me. All I cared about was learning the information I needed to know. Unfortunately, for that to happen, I needed to gain Ruby's trust. I felt up for the challenge, though. *I'll do whatever it takes to get what I want from these assholes.* "What did it feel like?" I asked suddenly. "What did it feel like when you killed those vampires last night?"

All three of them turned to look at me.

Ruby looked away, her brows slowly pulling together.

I assumed she was recalling what had happened.

"It was like a living death," she answered in a low voice. "I could see death, smell it, and taste it. That's all these creatures are—death and hunger."

"The Bleeders, at least," I clarified.

She gave me a confused look. "Bleeders or the Queen... it doesn't matter. That's what they all are. Look around you; they are killing the world. What happens after humans (and maybe even other supernaturals) cease to exist? What happens then?"

I didn't say anything, and neither did the others. "I'm going to take a piss," I announced as I threw my bag over my shoulder. "Don't think about leaving me behind."

"Make it quick because we just might," Axel shot back. He might not be brooding anymore, but the asshole part of him was still alive and well.

I continued walking in silence until I knew I was out of their hearing range. Then I quickly removed my bag and the small solar phone inside. I held it up to the sun, my eyes darting around the forest as the screen flashed, the sun's rays powering the device.

It finally came on, and I dialed the only number saved. "What the fuck were you thinking?" I whispered as soon as the person answered. "This was not what we talked about."

"Hello, Olcan," the vampire General's deep voice replied calmly on the other line. His words were said slowly and nonchalantly.

His tone pissed me off even more. "I lost all my men! All of them! I told you to wait and I'd give you the girl." I clenched my fist, my rage increasing. "Why didn't you just take her? The Bleeders weren't necessary!"

He sighed. "Plans change, Olcan. The Queen gave her orders,

and I obeyed them. Or do you no longer want to be a part of an alliance with her? It was your idea, after all."

I released my fist and exhaled as I pinched the bridge of my nose. "The deal with the Queen was that she'd allow me to find the girl and hand her over. In return, I'd be given Ruby's powers, or did the Queen lie about knowing how to do that?"

I pulled the phone away from my ear as the General hissed.

"Be careful of your words, wolf."

"Why didn't you just take her? You saw what she did. She's growing stronger. The Queen won't be able to—"

"To what?" he interjected, his voice coming out as a low hiss once more. "To kill her? Keep traveling with the girl, Olcan. Follow her to where the humans are, and report the location to me." He hung up.

I had to hold myself back from crushing the phone. I turned it off and threw it into my bag before covering my face with my hands. For years, I'd served as a Council member, and what did I have to show for it?

The other Council members, the self-righteous pricks, were too damn stuck up and trapped in the past to think long term. For years, I'd been telling them we needed to find a way to harness the Enchanteds' power and transfer it to other wolves that could transform. This would bring all werewolves closer to the Goddess, benefitting the entire werewolf society instead of just a few werewolf hybrids. Just thinking about how much stronger werewolves could become if our warriors had Enchanted powers sent chills down my spine.

Even though werewolves aged slower than humans, Enchanteds aged even more slowly, much like witches. In fact, before the truth of the Enchanteds' relationship to the Goddess was revealed, we actually thought Enchanteds descended from a werewolf bloodline tainted by witches.

If I had known from the beginning who Ruby was, the power she had...

My thoughts trailed off as a twig snapped within the forest, and I froze. I picked up my bag slowly as I listened for a heartbeat. The moment I heard it, I looked up and was engulfed by a cloud of black smoke.

• • • ⊷●● ●●⊶ • • •

XAVIER

"Hey!" Ruby called. "What's wrong?"

I turned my back on the forest as I faced her. "Nothing," I responded. "I thought I heard something."

"Why is Olcan taking so long?" She groaned as she got up off the ground, brushing her hand down the back of her pants.

My eyes drifted to Axel.

He was staring at her ass, then his hazel eyes wandered to me as he arched a brow.

I shook my head as I turned back to the forest. I couldn't fault him for enjoying the view.

"How far does he need to go to take a piss? I can't even hear his heartbeat," Axel said with annoyance. "I'm going to go find..." His words trailed off.

I turned to look at him. "Oh, I hear his—wait, there are two heartbeats."

Suddenly, a man fell from above and all three of us stepped back. It didn't take long before I realized it was Olcan crawling away on his arms to get away from the black smoke above him.

"Malcolm? What the hell are you doing?" Ruby yelled in shock.

Malcolm materialized out of the smoke. His red hair looked tousled and messy, his face red with anger. He pointed at Olcan on the ground. "You should ask him what he's doing, or what he's already done, for that matter."

"What are you talking about?" I asked.

Olcan got to his feet, his backpack falling off his shoulder. "Who the hell is this? Do you know who I am, boy?"

Malcolm's eyes narrowed. "Boy?"

"Olcan, meet my father." Ruby waved her hand from one man to the other. "Malcolm, meet Olcan, a member of the Werewolf Council. Now you both know each other, so what the hell is going on?"

"Your father's a demon?" Olcan inquired with his eyes wide. "How is that possible?"

"He was human. He made a deal with a demon," Axel told him as he stepped forward, his arms crossed over his chest. "That's not important right now. Malcolm, why did you do that?"

"He was speaking to someone in the forest." Malcolm pinned Olcan with a glare.

Now, all the color drained from Olcan's face.

"He was talking about Ruby, that they should have taken her, and that losing his men wasn't a part of their deal." Malcolm turned to Olcan, his jaws clenched. "This Council member is working with the vampires."

Axel was the first to act. He immediately charged at Olcan.

Olcan was quick, grabbing him by the shoulder and throwing him on the ground.

I barreled into Olcan with all the strength in my body. I climbed onto him quickly, my claws piercing into the sides of his neck while Malcolm trapped his left arm above his head and his legs.

"Move and I fucking kill you!" I barked in his face.

He stopped moving, but his right hand remained holding my wrist.

"You backstabbing little parasite! You betrayed us... betrayed your own kind!" I added, my face inches away from his.

"My own kind resents me!" he yelled back, his voice strained from my grip on his throat.

"Whose fault do you think that is, Olcan? What did you think would happen over time when you kept fucking everyone over like this?" Ruby asked him. "Your men getting killed last night is on you. Those men thought they could trust you... How could you?"

I tightened my hold on him. "What have you told the vampires? It was you, wasn't it? You gave them pack locations! You've been helping them with slaughtering the people you're meant to protect!"

He groaned. "You know nothing! You can't help someone that doesn't want to be helped!" he bit back. "I've tried for years to help our species, but you fools are just so stuck in your ways. Secluding ourselves from other species, not evolving, not becoming more powerful will be the end of us. We could all be like her. Don't you get it?"

"You'll never be like her," I yelled.

He clenched his jaws, his lips forming a thin line.

I could see the hatred in his eyes, and I knew he could see the same in mine. "Where is the Queen? What did she promise you?"

"You want the truth, young Alpha? I don't know where she is, but your pack was to be next," he whispered as he tried to ease himself up off the ground.

I pushed him back down.

Olcan winced as blood began to pour from the hole in his neck created by my claw. "Your father has always stood against me," he choked out. "The vampires were helping me to rid myself of anyone who stands against me and my plans. In the vampire's new world, the wolves that stand with me will be more powerful than ever! That's the deal I made with them."

How had this man remained on the Council for all these years?

"Natalie and my father, where are they?"

He smirked.

I punched the ground beside his head, my fangs elongating. "Where are they?" I yelled, my saliva spraying onto his face. "If you found us, you must have found them. I swear to the Goddess, if you've hurt them..." I picked him up by his throat and slammed him back down to the ground, the sound of breaking bones filling my ears. "Where are they?"

He closed his eyes as he started coughing. "They weren't there. When we got there, they were long gone. All of them—the entire pack was gone."

My hand loosened around his neck, but that was what he had been waiting for. Quickly, his hand holding my wrist transformed. He clawed me across my face, and I howled in pain as I fell back.

The rest of his transformation came quick, but so did Axel's as Olcan overpowered Malcolm's mist and broke free. Axel's black wolf tackled him back to the ground, both of them still mid-shift.

"Take Ruby!" I barked at Malcolm.

He nodded to me.

"The fuck he will!" she yelled in response.

With the cut on my face burning and my anger igniting my insides, I wasn't interested in dealing with Ruby's stubbornness. I waited for an opening and ran forward. I fell on the ground to slide between both Axel and Olcan. I ignored the stones cutting into my skin as I reached out and embedded my claws in Olcan's underbelly.

He recoiled in pain, his brown wolf limping as he tried to remain standing. He snarled at us, and since I was still on the ground, I could see his underbelly already healing.

Axel's black wolf growled in response, blood dripping from a deep bite on his front right leg. Olcan was experienced, so even with the two of us, taking him down would be difficult. I got to my feet quickly and ripped my shirt off my body.

Realizing I was about to shift, Olcan targeted me, foam at the sides of his mouth. As he came at me, his eyes shifted from black to their original color.

I knew he did it so I could see the hatred within them, his intent to kill.

Since it was too late to stop the shift, my right shoulder

dislocated. A wolf is most vulnerable mid-shift, so Axel rushed forward to protect me.

What we didn't expect was a tree limb from above reaching down to wrap around Olcan's body. It yanked him back, and his body slammed against the tree's trunk. More branches began to wrap around him, pinning him where he was.

Now, I looked Ruby's way.

Her hands were outstretched in front of her and shaking, her eyes as black as tar. She closed her eyes, her face turning red with strain as black veins began to crawl up her arms and Olcan's bones started to break.

His gut-wrenching howls of pain were cutting through the silence around us, and all we could do was stand and watch.

She was controlling his wolf as she had done before, forcing him to change back to his human form. When he had changed enough to speak, he began screaming her name.

I walked forward as I slowly commanded my shift to revert.

Axel started changing back as well.

"You were going to kill my father," I accused as I stopped in front of Olcan, droplets of blood rolling down his body from where the branches cut into his skin. "You almost got us killed—Ruby killed. Even worse, you betrayed your oath as a Council member."

He opened his mouth to speak, a smirk on his lips.

I reacted. My hand pierced through his chest easier than I had thought it would. Inside his body was burning hot. I closed my eyes as I ripped his heart from his chest.

I'd been soft for too long. Maybe Olcan hadn't lied about my father and Natalie having left before he arrived. Even so, if I let him go—if we let him go—he would only try to kill us another day.

He would only try to kill Ruby another day, and that I wouldn't stand for.

CHAPTER SEVEN
RUBY

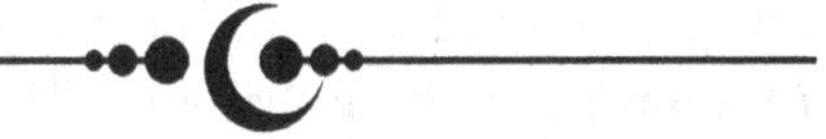

We walked until almost sunset when we made our way off the road and into the forest. First, we had planned to camp outside with the guys taking turns keeping watch. Then we found an abandoned house and decided to sleep there for the night, instead.

The dilapidated house didn't offer much cover from a vampire attack with broken windows and rotting doors, but it was better than sleeping outside.

Since Malcolm was with us, he agreed to set wards around the house for the night to hide our location and mask my scent.

So far, Malcolm's wards seemed to be the only thing capable of blocking my scent. I couldn't walk around with a ward in my pocket, and yes... I had asked if I could. Sadly, wards could only be set if I was inside a structure.

The guys locked me inside the house while they did a quick sweep of the forest before nightfall. It took me a while to find a spot in the dirty house to lie down comfortably while I waited for them to return. There was an old mattress at the other end of the room, but the odors coming from it were beyond questionable.

To be honest, the entire little house gave me the creeps. Who the hell decided to live all the way out in the middle of nowhere?

The soft squeak of a mouse met my ears. The little critter ran by me and headed for the door. I watched as his tiny body slipped through a hole in the door, and I smiled. He had no idea what was going on in the world. This house and the surrounding forest was his entire little universe.

I closed my tired eyes and immediately saw Olcan's face in my mind. What happened to a person to make them become so selfish? Or was he just born that way? I'd never understood how some people could ruin others' lives just to make themselves feel better or improve their own lives. Olcan was fine with his people being massacred and turned into monsters just as long as he got what he wanted.

I understand Olcan thought what he did was right. He thought making a deal with the devil was better than watching his species be slaughtered, and he believed werewolves would be made stronger in the process. The problem came when he decided to double-cross and sacrifice everyone else who didn't agree. Countless wolves must've lost their lives thanks to his betrayal.

In the beginning, I wanted to run away from all of this. I didn't know what I was or where I came from. Yet, knowing now that I could help save the lives of so many people, how could I not do my part?

It did feel scary, and I didn't know what might happen at any given moment. Yet, if I could save a single life, it'd be worth it. I opened my eyes and held my hand up in front of my face. I had to become stronger. I had to find out what my limits were. It seemed as if I was capable of anything, everything, but I knew I must have had limits. I wasn't a god, and I wasn't immortal. However, I felt this wave of invincibility whenever I called on my power, and it scared me. I'd realized that the more I used my powers, the easier it was becoming to control them.

Olcan said something to me that I hadn't been able to stop

thinking about. He'd said, *"In war, control isn't the most important thing. In war, we have to break ourselves free from the restrictions of doubt that could hold us back. We have to do what needs to be done because our opponents will do anything to win."*

Too bad Olcan took that a bit too far. I thought werewolves were big on honor, but Olcan had none at all.

Despite everything Olcan had done, I hadn't expected Xavier to kill him. If anything, I had expected Axel to do it. If Axel had been the one to kill him, it wouldn't have been so shocking. Xavier... Xavier was someone else a few hours ago. At that moment, when he stuck his hand into Olcan's chest, my own heart had stopped beating. I'd only seen Xavier kill one other werewolf. He had killed a suicidal werewolf months ago when we just met. Last night was the first time since then that I'd seen him in such a dark place.

We had walked in silence for hours afterward. I think both Axel and Malcolm were shocked as well.

I believe everything happening to all of us would hit a breaking point sooner or later. As Xavier walked away from Olcan's lifeless body still strapped to the tree, his face was utterly devoid of emotion. I didn't see regret or even anger.

An old, discolored glass sitting on the tiny kitchen counter across the room fell to the ground and shattered. My hand flew to my mouth to stop the scream that rolled up my throat. I got up quickly and looked through one of the windows. The world was growing dark outside, and still, the guys hadn't returned.

"Where are you guys?" I whispered to myself as I glanced back at the broken glass on the floor. There were no lights inside the house, so as night drew closer, the place got darker. I couldn't see in the dark like Axel and Xavier. I walked to the door but decided against going outside. I'd rather be stuck in here with a ghost than attacked by a vampire out there. "Hurry back," I whispered. "This place is really starting to creep me out."

AXEL

"We should head back now," Xavier told me.

I turned around as Malcolm appeared by our side.

I fanned at the black mist in front of my face and shot him an annoyed look.

He merely shrugged and fell in stride with Xavier and me.

We walked in silence, but I was keeping an eye on Xavier. He had surprised me earlier. I hadn't thought he had it in him to kill Olcan. I couldn't believe he killed a Council member without blinking an eye. The bastard had it coming, that's for sure, though I did feel a little angry that I didn't get to end his pathetic life myself.

In the beginning, I didn't see Xavier as capable of becoming a strong Alpha, an Alpha who could make the tough decisions without showing remorse or regret. We were raised to be strong, resilient, and fearless—Alphas more so than other wolves. I saw him as weak because he fell for Ruby so quickly. Xavier hadn't questioned or fought against the mate bond and had left himself open to being used. Back then, I'd believed Ruby and our mate bond had to be some kind of trick or witchery.

Today I saw Xavier act as a true Alpha, not a young Alpha-to-be. I saw a brave and decisive Alpha who took the initiative and did a thing few would've had the courage to do. If allowed to live, Olcan would have stopped at nothing to kill Ruby and see his evil plan of vampire/werewolf alliance to fruition, and Xavier knew it.

"Do you think Olcan told the vampires about Presley, then?" I pondered.

"He did," Malcolm replied with a shrug. "He was told to report back once he'd found the base."

"That General will be following us," Xavier commented as he

stepped over a broken tree limb. "We're going to end up leading them straight to the humans."

"We don't have a choice," I shot back. "We have to go there, and it's too late to turn back now."

"I wasn't suggesting turning back, but once we get there, we need to let them know the vampires aren't far behind."

The forest around us got so quiet. It was unnerving. With nightfall upon us, I was used to hearing the insects as they came out for the night, but all I could hear was our footsteps. It was as if we were utterly alone in the world.

"I found something else in the book," Malcolm suddenly announced as he stopped walking. "It's why I came looking for you."

I frowned at the look of worry on his face. "What is it? What did you find?"

"This isn't the first time the vampires had done this," he announced. "That's what the war was that we saw in the book. They tried taking over a long time ago and were stopped."

"How?" Xavier asked the question I was thinking of.

Malcolm shook his head as he pinched the bridge of his nose.

"Malcolm?" I called to him.

He looked up at me, his hand falling to his side. "A werewolf sacrificed herself. She accepted the Goddess's power. While she ultimately defeated the vampires... it killed her," he finally answered.

My heart fell. "Are you saying Ruby will..."

He nodded. "Yes. That's what Ruby will have to do. She won't only use the power given to her by the Goddess, she'll become the Goddess."

Xavier walked away as he combed his hand through his hair roughly.

"Her body is what the Goddess wants." My voice dropped low with disbelief. "She gave Ruby her power from birth to groom her for this, for when she will have to take over her body."

The loud sound of a tree falling echoed through the forest.

I looked around.

Xavier's claws were retracting, a large claw mark across the tree's trunk. "No," he growled, his shoulder tense. He turned to face us, his eyes black as coal. "The Goddess can possess someone else. Not her."

"There has to be another way," I told Malcolm, my heartbeat pounding in my ears at the thought of losing Ruby. "Not her, I can't lose her too."

"I'm telling you what I know!" Malcolm tossed his hands up in frustration. "That's all. Dammit, I don't want this either! She's my only daughter. Yet Ruby is also the perfect candidate. She was born an Enchanted with a part of the Goddess already inside her. All the Goddess had to do was give her more—a higher dose of her divinity, if you will." He walked away, his head down. "There's a tiny possibility she might not die... maybe the Goddess did this to avoid killing her. The werewolf who died before wasn't an Enchanted."

"This is fucking bullshit!" I yelled. "Isn't the vampire Queen just another supernatural being like us? Why does it take a god to kill her, huh? Even though Ruby was born half Enchanted, you know hosts possessed by gods never last long. Mortals aren't built to host or wield the powers of divine beings. Ruby won't survive this!" I looked at Xavier, my eyes wide with panic. "She won't survive it, no matter how strong she is now. Ruby's been lucky to have survived this long. You saw what happened when she killed those vampires the other night. She almost died! Just like before, her powers almost burned her to death!"

"We can't tell her about this," Malcolm stated resolutely as he turned around. "This fight isn't hers alone, so killing the Queen isn't her job or duty alone. She won't have to accept the Goddess if she doesn't even know it's possible to do so."

"Okay." Xavier sighed as he walked forward. There was no color in his face. "She doesn't learn of this. We'll find Presley, work with the humans, and stop this from ever coming to pass. The first time this happened, the world wasn't as advanced as it is now. We'll find another way."

I knew he was feeling the panic I was. "And what if there is no other way?" I asked as I clenched my fists so hard I felt my nails pierce into my skin. "What if Ruby has to accept the Goddess in the end?"

"Then she'll just have to, and we'll lose her. It means we have failed to protect her as we should have." Malcolm replied softly.

Releasing a frustrated breath, I stalked away.

"She can't do that!" Xavier yelled from somewhere behind me. "She can't!"

"If it gets to that point and she doesn't," Malcolm replied coolly, "We all die."

We walked back to the house in silence. Why did it take a goddess to kill the vampire Queen? How could she possibly be that powerful?

We found Ruby asleep in the corner of the shack, her legs curled up to her chest. She looked so small, so fragile, and perfect. Her pink rosebud lips were parted somewhat, her breathing slow.

I inhaled her scent and lost it. I couldn't take it. I couldn't handle looking at her while knowing I might lose her. I stormed out of the house, shifting as I ran.

"Axel!" Malcolm called.

I ran back into the forest, the black fur of my wolf bursting through my skin.

"Axel!"

<hr>

RUBY

I'm not sure what happened with the guys while they were in the forest last night, but they returned as new men. They were all so quiet, so distant and tense. I knew I was missing something, but what?

"What's going on?" I asked Xavier as I pulled up at his side, the midday sun causing sweat to break out on my upper lip.

He looked down at me and smiled, but it didn't quite meet his eyes. "What are you talking about?"

"I'm talking about why you're all so quiet and tense," I said loud enough for the others to hear, although I knew they could hear me just fine before. "You've all been acting strange since last night. What did I miss?"

"Nothing, Ruby," Xavier replied. "I think everyone just has a lot on their minds is all. I certainly do," he added quietly.

I realized I was being insensitive. I had hoped Natalie would finally appear to me while I slept last night, but there was still no word from her. "The warding around the camp was getting weak before we left. Maybe that's what drove them to leave."

"Yeah, maybe," he replied. "I hope so."

"You don't have an Enchanted in your pack, do you, Axel?" I stopped and waited for him and Malcolm to catch up.

Xavier kept walking, apparently lost in his thoughts.

"I don't." Axel shook his head. "But the witches have their ways to contact me if they need me," he confirmed, a few strands of curly hair in his face.

"Do you miss them?" I wondered as Malcolm walked ahead of us.

Axel nodded. "I do."

"Your father, how is he?" I questioned him.

His face fell. He sucked his bottom lip in and released it, as his teeth grazed the skin. His lip seemed so much plumper afterward. I looked away quickly as he stared down at me, no doubt hearing the way my heartbeat increased.

My stomach did a backflip as he held my hand.

"He was up and about when I left, but that feels like so long ago. The witches there have been helping him, so he's doing okay, I guess."

I nodded, his thumb caressing the back of my hand a sudden distraction. Axel and I didn't speak about his pack or past very often. With the way things had been, no one had the time to sit and chat.

I was mated to these two men, and sometimes it didn't feel like that. Although I was mated to Axel, we never talked about being officially together. Finding your mate meant finding the one you would spend the rest of your life with, but things got complicated when you were mated to two wolves instead of one. Xavier and I grew close from the start and made our relationship official, while Axel and I were still just finding our footing.

Although things were civil between both men, it still got awkward from time to time. There were more important things to think about right now, though, like... oh, I don't know—the world ending and the pressure of trying to save it.

I'd deal with this mess of a relationship when this was all over. For now, I'd enjoy their embrace, their words of encouragement, and the delectable kisses we stole from time to time. Yes, for now, I'd enjoy having two men by my side that I knew would do anything for me. I glanced up at Axel before looking at Xavier walking ahead. I'd do anything for them as well—anything.

Suddenly, Malcolm removed his coat and threw it in the air. The garment turned to smoke and vanished. If it came to it, I might make Malcolm suffer a little before helping him. He was an asshole sometimes, but I had to admit, his skills frequently came in handy. I hadn't fully forgiven him for wanting to kill me, but I certainly didn't want anything bad to happen to him. So yes, I'd save his sorry ass, too.

I smiled.

Look at me, talking about saving other people's asses. What is the world coming to?

"Wait," Axel suddenly commanded as his hold on my hand grew tighter.

Ahead of us, Xavier spun around and started pointing towards the forest for us to get off the road.

"What's going on?" I whispered to Axel as we ran quickly to the forest.

"Humans, we hear humans," Axel whispered as his eyes scanned the forest.

"Maybe it's Presley's men?" I whispered back.

Malcolm shifted into smoke and vanished.

Xavier pulled up at my side. "Or hunters," he countered and then nodded at Axel.

They both started removing their shirts. I chuckled at them speaking to each other without words. It was kind of hot, if you thought about it—my men having a private language centered around protecting me.

My wandering naughty thoughts were washed away as men rushed forward with guns aimed at us.

"Don't move!"

Commands kept flying at us from all angles.

"Hands up! Get your hands up now!"

"Don't even think about it, wolf!"

I held my hands up.

Xavier and Axel started to wolf out, their eyes changing as they snarled at the men, but they remained in human form.

"Stop! If you shift, we'll shoot!" one man yelled.

I placed my arm on Xavier's as he leaned forward somewhat, his ears elongating as a loud growl emitted from him. "Don't," I whispered to him. "Don't be the animal they think we are."

A burst of black smoke suddenly confused the men.

Axel, Xavier, and I stepped back to avoid being engulfed by it.

"Malcolm, no!" I shouted. Within the black cloud, we could hear men screaming while gunshots echoed around us. "I said stop, Malcolm! Stop it!"

The smoke disappeared and Malcolm materialized before us. Without warning, another gunshot echoed through the forest, and Malcolm staggered backward.

Presley stepped forward, his gun raised.

I ran forward and stood in front of Malcolm. "General Presley, don't shoot. Please listen!" I pleaded. "Please!"

He lowered his gun ever so slightly but then looked at Malcolm and raised it again. "You killed my men."

"They aren't dead. Check for yourself," Malcolm replied nonchalantly.

"Not these men, you motherfucker!" Presley yelled.

I turned around to face Malcolm. "Leave," I murmured to him. "You killed his men. Please, you need to leave. You can find us easily, can't you?"

Malcolm stared at me in shock, then he sighed. He burst into a cloud of smoke without another word.

I quickly turned back around to face Presley, who looked ready to murder someone. "Look, I support you wanting to shoot him again. Sometimes I feel the same way about him. In fact, I'll even cheer for you when you two finally get to fight it out, but not right now. I didn't know he would kill your men, okay? He was just trying to protect me. I'm sorry, I really am. I'm on your side, Presley." I lowered my raised hands as he lowered his gun.

More men appeared, their guns aimed at us.

"Stand down!" Presley yelled at them before turning to me.

"I need your help, and you need mine," I told him calmly.

He arched a brow at me. "What makes you think I still want your help?" he shot back.

I pinned him with a look. "You do, and you know it. The vampires are heading here. They're looking for you," I told him.

All the men started to exchange worried glances.

"We have a lot to talk about." I stepped forward. "I got my memories back," I revealed.

This news had his brows touching his hairline in surprise.

"Shall we go then?" I prompted.

***

RUBY

It took half an hour for us to get to Presley's base. The looks we received as we walked through the base's halls were a mixture of curiosity and outright disdain.

"I need to show you something," Presley announced as he pushed two double doors open and led us into a massive hall.

"Ruby!" Natalie screamed from across the room. Within seconds, she crossed the room to pull me into a hug.

"Natalie," I said softly as I squeezed her to me.

Behind her, the rest of the pack turned to see what was going on. Mathieu stood up, a wide smile making its way to his face.

"Dad?" Xavier called out in disbelief as he stepped away to greet his father.

Natalie pulled away, and we stared at each other for a moment before hugging each other again.

"I'm so glad you're okay," I confessed with a sigh as we released each other once more.

"I missed you, too," she replied before looking at Axel. "Even you."

Axel chuckled. "I can't say the same."

Natalie flipped him off as he walked away.

"Come on." She took my hand. "They've been asking for you."

"Who?" I asked.

She stared at me as if I was crazy. "The pack, of course. We've all been worried sick about you guys," she replied as if it should've been obvious to me.

I frowned.

In the beginning, the pack blamed me for being on the run, and the animosity was palpable. However, by the time I left the pack with Presley, the dislike had started to fade as they realized there was a war being fought on all fronts. I was being hunted by The Council and vampires, not to mention the human hunters. "That's, um, good… I think. I'll be right there."

Natalie looked at Presley, who stood by the door, and nodded to him before turning away. Then she jumped onto Xavier's back and they hugged as Mathieu patted his son's shoulder.

A little girl waved at me with a small, timid smile on her lips.

I smiled wide as I waved back at her.

"The strangest thing happened to me," Presley began as he moved to stand next to me. "Natalie appeared to me in a dream, saying she needed my help." He turned to face me, his hands clasped behind his back. His chestnut-blonde hair seemed longer than it was the last time I saw him, and his blue eyes seemed paler. His eyes still seemed just as unreadable as ever. "She told me you'd come to find me soon."

I puckered my lips as I looked Natalie's way. "She saw a vision of this happening, I guess." I continued watching her as she spoke animatedly to Xavier. Xavier wore a large grin, and his shoulders appeared more relaxed. I smiled broadly.

"She told me the warding around her camp was weakening. She knew they'd be attacked soon, so she needed my help until you came to find me," Presley stated.

I swung my gaze over to him. "And you helped them, just like that? Aren't the people you report to mad that you have an entire werewolf pack here when you should be hunting werewolves?"

"Like I had told you before, my team doesn't hunt werewolves. I'm on your side, Ruby. Never forget that. So, yes, I helped her." He glanced Natalie's way.

I narrowed my eyes as his eyes lingered on her a little too long. I tried to hide my smile.

He turned back to me. "The sooner we get started, the better."

I nodded as I inhaled deeply and sighed. "I know. Just give me a few minutes, okay?"

"Sure, I'll let you catch up with your family. I'll be back soon." He strode away, closing the doors behind him.

I turned around to find Mathieu calling me over. *My family*, I thought to myself as I joined them. It was nice to hear someone say that.

Mathieu patted me on the shoulder as the little girl from before handed me a glass of water.

"Thank you," I replied to her.

She beamed at me before running back to her mother.

The other wolves were all looking at me strangely. I bumped Natalie with my elbow, "Am I missing something? Why is everyone looking at me like that?"

"I had a vision of you killing more vampires. I told them all about it," she whispered back. "That actually happened, right?"

I nodded. "Oh, so much happened, so much." I sat down, as did everyone else.

Axel, Xavier, and I told them about everything that had happened, from the beginning.

Everyone looked particularly shocked to hear that Xavier was the one who killed Olcan.

"That backstabbing prick," Natalie snarled through clenched teeth. "I haven't been able to contact Reika. He must have killed her. Maybe he found out she was on our side or that she had helped you guys escape from the pack when he wanted to take you guys to Romania."

"Maybe," Mathieu replied, his dark hair like Xavier's but longer while brushing against his shoulder. "Did he say anything about the other council members?"

Xavier shook his head. "He didn't."

Axel excused himself, saying he was going to get something to eat.

Mathieu offered to show both Axel and Xavier where the cafeteria was.

"So," I drawled as I turned to face Natalie. "You mind-linked Presley, huh?"

The smile appearing on her lips was the one I'd hoped to see. So I hadn't been wrong about the chemistry I'd been sensing between those two. Presley had looked at Natalie in the same way I'd seen Xavier and Axel look at me.

"I did. He was the only person I could think about to help us," she admitted. "We were going to be killed. I wish I had seen that Olcan was behind it all, though."

"I'm just glad you guys are okay. Xavier was starting to worry," I told her.

The door to the hall opened again.

I sighed.

Presley made his way over to us, his eyes on Natalie for a moment before he looked at me. He finally came to a stop at our table. "Ruby, it's time. We need to get started."

"Alright." I pushed my chair back.

Natalie got up with me and pulled me into a hug.

So much tension that I'd been holding in for days finally faded away. "We'll talk when I get finished, okay?"

She nodded before pulling away.

I then followed Presley out the door and down the hall. "Where are we going?"

"You're about to meet 'the people I report to,' as you called them."

"This isn't going to be fun?" I asked dryly.

Presley shook his head without looking behind him. "I doubt it."

CHAPTER EIGHT
RUBY

I walked behind Presley in silence, observing and absorbing everything I saw.

People were walking quickly back and forth, all seeming to be in a rush, while we walked casually. Three times we were stopped as Presley was asked to sign a document and god knows what else.

People kept giving me odd looks.

I tried to ignore them, but it was starting to bother me. I'd never enjoyed being the center of attention.

"They've all heard what you're capable of," Presley voiced as he kept walking ahead of me. "We're happy you've decided to help us."

"Whatever it takes to get these vampires," I responded.

He remained silent.

After several minutes, we came to large white double doors.

Presley placed his hand on a scanner and the door unlocked for him.

We stepped inside the room and I immediately had to take a step back as a woman walked in front of me, a stack of files in her hand.

The sizable room seemed filled with computers and so many soldiers. At the other end of the room, a wall stood covered in large screens, all showing something different.

I understood none of it.

"This is where the magic happens," Presley said loudly as he marched forward.

While he stepped straight forward freely and confidently, I had to dodge and weave to avoid bumping into people.

He stopped at a desk with a woman typing away quickly at her keyboard, her eyes darting back and forth between the three computer monitors before her. "We think we've found the Queen."

My jaw dropped with shock. "What? How? Are you sure?"

"We've been able to hunt these vampires—finding their covens and all—because we've modified one of our satellites to pick up on areas devoid of heat signatures. Vampires don't have a heat signature. We think it's their skin that causes it, much as if a human put on an insulated jacket. We discovered this when a diplomat had to be located by satellite. We noticed the dense dark zones around his house and realized it was surrounded by vampires. So, wherever you see a large dark spot..." He pointed to a screen across the room of what indeed looked like a map of America but with multiple black spots. "...that's where the vampires are."

"That's a lot," I murmured more to myself than him.

"It is," he agreed.

The map was almost completely covered. While some black areas were larger than others, it was discouraging to see a visual representation of how quickly and completely the vampires were taking over the United States. If America looked this bad, I didn't want to think about what the rest of the world looked like.

"Show her," Presley stated while pointing to one of the monitors on the lady's desk. "There, that large black area... it's one of the larger ones we've located. There are a few human heat signatures." He turned to me. "We sent in a team to do recon on the area, and we got footage of what looked like a female vampire surrounded by guards being led inside an old building."

"How do you know it's her from just getting a glimpse of a female vampire?" I inquired. "We have no idea what the Queen looks like, or if she even looks human."

"That's true," Presley agreed with a nod, his arms clasped behind him as usual. "But whoever that woman was, the fact that she was so heavily guarded suggests she has to be important."

"Okay, what do you want me to do, then? I assume you want me to do something."

He nodded. "I do. I want you to join the team I'll be leading. Come with us to that location. We don't know if it's the Queen, but if it is, we'll need you there."

At this point, several soldiers had stopped what they were doing to listen to our conversation. Actually, they were all just staring at me.

The noise in the room decreased as Presley waited for my response—as they all waited.

"Yes, sure," I agreed, sounding a lot more confident than I actually felt.

Everyone resumed work with great haste.

There were still others staring at me, but they didn't bother me much. I'd decided if this was where I needed to be from now on, I had to get used to being in the spotlight for a little while. Eventually, they would all just get used to seeing me around, and hopefully the extra attention would fade.

Presley cocked his head to the side. "Come with me." He moved away. "Time to meet the others. They want to see your power for themselves, if you're truly capable of killing vampires."

I hurried to catch up with him.

He placed his hand on another scanner, this time for an elevator.

We stepped inside, and I wondered if the guys could hear my

pounding heart wherever they were. Yup, I was freaking out. I had no idea what I would even say to these people or do.

We rode the elevator in silence to Floor D3. I exhaled as the doors opened.

Presley walked out.

I followed him.

A long hall loomed ahead of us with a door at the other end, and once more his hand was the key to opening the door.

The moment the door opened, I heard it—the unmistakable hiss of a vampire. My body grew tense as I stepped into the room. Sure enough, there was a vampire—a Bleeder to be exact—chained in a glass box.

The room was all white, with three televisions to my right. Two men that looked like doctors were in what looked like an observation room to my left. The Bleeder's red eyes landed on me and it rushed towards me at full speed until its chain yanked it back. Bright UV lights switched on inside the box and the creature began to scream in pain, something like steam rising off its skin.

The UV lights turned off once more, and the Bleeder cowered in a corner, its crimson eyes still trained on me.

"Hello, Ms. Saunders," a woman's voice echoed in the room.

I looked towards the televisions that had been off when we came in.

They were now on, with the silhouette of a man on the first and third television screen. A woman with chocolate brown skin and black eyes appeared on the one in the middle.

"Hi," I drawled.

The woman smiled. "It's nice to finally meet you, Ruby. May I call you Ruby?"

"Sure," I replied. "And you are?"

"I'm Rebecca," she told me. "My associates would rather remain anonymous. You understand."

I looked at the other two screens, then glanced at Presley as I shook my head. "Not really, but okay."

She gave me a little nod and clasped her hands on the glass desk before her. "We've heard many things about you over these past few months. You have a gift that General Presley says is vital to our efforts to destroy these creatures." She gestured with her hand towards the vampire in the cage.

It hissed back at her in response.

She didn't even flinch, and her eyes drifted back to me. "What General Presley hasn't been able to confirm for us, however, is exactly what you are," she added as she smiled.

Though her smile was quite beautiful, I knew it was fake. It looked like something she'd practiced and forced for so long that now, maybe to her, it even felt real.

"I'm half-human," I replied, "And half-Enchanted."

"Enchanted?" one of the men repeated.

I could not tell which one spoke as I answered, "Yes." I stared at both men.

Rebecca was nodding her head. "Yes, that's right. Within the werewolf species, they have Enchanteds, female wolves that can't transform. Yes?" She leaned forward, her eyes narrowing. "So any hybrid children of an Enchanted and human would have the gifts you do, then?"

"No," I told her. "They wouldn't. My gifts are unique in the supernatural community as well."

"Ruby," Presley spoke as he turned to face me, "we would like you to kill that Bleeder. Show us what you're capable of."

The Bleeder seemed to understand everything being said as he stood up. He hunched forward somewhat, his eyes now darting back and forth frantically. He hissed at us, saliva draining from his mouth. The pale creature ran forward, but once more the chain around his thin left ankle yanked him back, and the UV lights switched on. He fell to the ground in agony again, his hands covering his bald head as steam rose from its body. The light switched off, and the creature continued to whimper like a dog on the ground. The way he was curled up, looking so fragile and helpless, I felt a pang of pity for him.

Whoever this man once was, he didn't ask to be turned into this creature.

"That's not a being deserving of pity, Ruby," Presley whispered to me. "Not anymore."

The vampire held his head up then, his eyes on Presley.

I tilted my head to the side as I watched him get onto his knees.

The Bleeder held its head back as if smelling the air. "F-fil-ty," he stuttered hesitantly, the word coming out in pieces.

Presley's eyes grew wide for a moment.

"F-fil-ty hu-man," the Bleeder finally managed to utter.

"It's never spoken before," Presley noted.

The vampire smiled wide, his eyes drifting to me.

I hadn't known Bleeders were still capable of speech. The Skins, like the General I had seen, were the vampires who carried on conversations, exhibited logical thought, and could still pass for human.

"Y-ou... die," the vampire hissed at me as his black tongue darted out to lick his lips. "Queen w-w-will..." He shook his head. "Kill... y-y-you. Make... o-one of of... us."

"It's saying the Queen wants to make you one of them," Presley clarified as he unclasped his hands from behind him and crossed them over his chest.

"I know," I told him and stepped closer to the cage. "Where have you all been?" I asked the vampire.

He started laughing, a contorted sound as if he was also coughing.

"If your Queen wants me, tell me where she is, so I can go to her."

His laughter grew louder.

I clenched my jaw as I felt my power awake within me. "Tell me!"

"Blo-blood," he replied in a low hiss. "B-lood, blood, blood."

His face began to twist as if he were in pain, and he tried to crawl closer to the glass. He started to chant the word, and he grew clearer each time he said it.

"Tell me where your Queen is, and I'll give you blood."

"Ruby." Presley's voice vibrated with concern.

I ignored him and pressed my wrist against the glass.

"Tell me where your Queen is, and I'll give you blood. Tell me."

He started shaking his head wildly and suddenly lashed out with so much force, a link on the chain opened and snapped.

Presley stepped back, and a blazing alarm went off inside the room.

The vampire started banging on the glass wall, and the UV light within the box came on.

"Turn it off!" I yelled to the people within the observation room. "I said turn it off!" I shouted again, my eyes turning black, and the light switched off.

The moment the light switched off, the vampire attacked himself, biting out a chunk of flesh from his arm.

I held my hand out, imagining myself holding the vampire by the throat and within the cage.

He lifted off the ground. He started clawing at his throat.

I raised my other hand, restricting his movement further. "Tell me where she is or die," I demanded.

The Bleeder's red eyes bulged as if they'd pop from his head. "Die," he screeched out.

I ground my teeth. "So be it," I stated and allowed it to fall to the ground. I imagined a flame being lit inside his body.

He instantly began to wither and twist on the ground. His body folded backward, his head almost touching his waist as the surface of his skin began to burn.

Presley stepped forward as the vampire slowly started to writhe less, and then stopped moving altogether, his body turning to ash.

The alarm in the room went silent.

I turned to Rebecca and the men, who'd been watching the entire thing. I stepped closer to the televisions, my eyes still as black as obsidian. "You have your proof, but I will only help you if you stop hunting werewolves." I straightened my spine and channeled the dominance I'd seen Xavier and Axel display. "Then, and only then, will I help you. Werewolves must be able to come out of hiding safely so they can help us in this fight. What you all don't understand is that this isn't the first time vampires have tried to take this world, and a werewolf was ultimately responsible for defeating the vampires in the previous fight. We can't win this war divided, and you're all fools if you think you can."

Rebecca's chest rose as she inhaled deeply.

I went on, "This world doesn't belong to humans alone. It never has, and it never will. This is *our* home—every creature, human and otherwise. Humans don't have the skill or strength to hunt these vampires the way werewolves do. It doesn't matter how many guns or bombs you have in your arsenal. So..." I crossed my arms over my chest. "That's my condition. Do we have a deal or not?"

Rebecca stared at me.

I held her stare. I would not back down or show weakness. I knew my eyes were still black, and I wasn't about to change them back to make the humans comfortable. I might be human, but I was an Enchanted as well. My mother was an incredibly gifted Enchanted who helped the werewolf community and made her mark in the supernatural world. I was my mother's daughter after all, and I would make my mark as well.

"Okay, Ruby," Rebecca agreed as she leaned forward. This time when she smiled, it met her eyes. "We have a deal."

RUBY

"I'm proud of you." Natalie threw her arm around my shoulder. "It definitely sounds like you handled it like a boss. I taught you well."

"*You* taught me well?" I told her with a laugh.

She nodded. "Of course I did. It sure as hell wasn't those two knuckleheads!" She pointed at Xavier and Axel walking ahead of us. "Are you really sure they're going to stop the hunting werewolves, though?"

I nodded. "I'm sure."

"And the Queen?"

Xavier and Axel halted their steps at the same time to look around at me.

"Don't even say it," I told them. "Presley wants me there, so I'm going. Neither of you can burn vampires alive with your mind, can you?"

Neither of them answered me.

I shrugged. "Then I have to go. You're both acting like you won't be there anyway."

"I just hope it was really the Queen," Natalie said. "It'd be good to get this nightmare over with. To be frank, I'm not the slightest bit upset that I won't be able to come. I'll leave this fight up to the pros." She patted my shoulder. "Just make sure you all come back in one piece."

"I'm not a pro." I stepped towards the door leading to the training room. "All I have is some power. I don't know the first thing about actual combat, like the hand-to-hand type stuff."

"I'd suggest you not worry about that," Axel stated. "With your power, a vampire shouldn't be able to get close enough. Leave the rest to us." He stepped forward, pinched my chin, and pushed the door to the training room open.

Xavier moved close, kissed the top of my head, and entered behind Axel.

The door closed softly, and I looked over at Natalie.

She was staring at me with puppy dog eyes. "That was so cute.

They are so cute. I'm liking this two-mates thing." She raised her head up to the ceiling. "Goddess, I've seen what you've done for others and—"

I yanked her hand. "Shut up and come on."

We entered the training room and found everyone staring in our direction. The room fell completely silent. All the soldiers stopped what they were doing. The tension and animosity in the room was stifling.

Axel and Xavier walked over to a barbell set like they owned the place.

Everyone, including Natalie and me, watched as Axel stacked all the weights onto a bar and lifted it with ease.

He made a face as he placed it back onto the ground with one hand. "Maybe we should just spar," he suggested to Xavier as he removed his shirt.

Xavier smirked. "It's been a long time coming."

A loud clunk echoed through the room.

All eyes turned to a man who'd dropped a dumbbell, his eyes on Xavier and Axel.

"Hmm, the love in this room is strong," Natalie said sarcastically. "Oh, here we go," she added as the man started making his way over to Xavier and Axel, his bare chest glistening with sweat.

Natalie and I joined them.

"Hey, guys, look what we have here. It's our new best friends, the werewolves," the soldier began. "So, I heard you guys can't transform on a full moon. That sucks."

"Jack, don't," another man cautioned him.

Jack smiled and shrugged his shoulders. "Hey, I'm only making conversation." He then turned back to Xavier and Axel.

This man was looking for trouble. For sure, he intended to piss Axel or Xavier off, and then shit was going to hit the fan. I could see it happening already.

"Literally every story about werewolves says they transform on a full moon."

"Do you believe every story you've ever heard?" Natalie questioned him with a sweet smile, but I could hear the distaste in her voice. She leaned forward.

Jack arched a brow at her. From the way he looked her up and down, I guessed the fact that she was gorgeous hadn't escaped him.

"So, I guess you believe in Santa Claus, too?" she asked him.

"Are you about to tell me he's real?" he asked her.

She shrugged. "He might be. Who knows?"

Jack turned back to Axel. "That was pretty impressive with the barbell and all. So..." He stepped closer as he narrowed his eyes at Axel. "Our team doesn't hunt werewolves, so I've never seen one of you guys wolf out. I hear it's pretty amazing."

A few men chuckled behind him.

This seemed to fuel his ego as he started laughing. "How about you show us those black eyes, freak?"

The corner of Axel's mouth arched with a smirk.

I stepped forward. "How about I show you mine?" I offered as I stepped in front of Axel, my eyes having changed from green to black. "*Pretty amazing, right*?" I said it the same sarcastic way he had.

He made a face. "Yeah, but I wasn't talking to you, sweetheart. I was talking to your little boyfriend behind you, or can he not speak for himself?" He peered behind me at Axel. "So, can you speak?" He looked at Xavier as well. "Either of you?"

"Hey!" I snapped my finger at him. "Back off."

He peered back down at me, then chuckled and held his hand up as he looked back at his friends. "Just having some fun, honey. Calm down."

"Don't... call me 'honey', asshat," I told him through clenched teeth.

He frowned as it started to get hot in the room. He looked me up and down, the smartass look on his face vanishing.

I could see him attempting to hide his fear.

Typical bully.

I stepped forward.

Xavier, Natalie, and Axel stepped back.

Sweat started to drip from Jack's face.

"So, I see no one has told you bullying isn't nice, no matter the age. I don't like bullies."

He kept stepping back when another taller soldier appeared behind him. He placed his hand on Jack's shoulders and tugged him further back. "Leave them alone."

Jack sent us a look of utter repulsion. "Gladly," he snapped as he walked away.

I rolled my eyes which turned back to my regular emerald green.

"Sorry about him. He's not the brightest bulb we have here." The tall soldier held his hand out to me. "I'm Alonzo. You're Ruby, right?"

I shook his hand. "I am. How'd you know?"

"Come on... redhead that can burn vampires with a look... of course I know who you are! We all do." He released my hand. "Plus, I think everyone just felt how hot it got in here." He looked at the guys behind me. "I don't think the equipment we have in here will work for you guys, but we'll work something out."

"Work it out how?" Xavier questioned.

Alonzo pinched his chin. "How about a fair fight between one of you and one of us? Of course, you'd have to go easy on us but—"

"No thanks," Axel answered quickly.

Alonzo frowned. "Why not? Trust me, I'm not like those guys. I just think it would be cool."

"No, we get what you mean, but us going easy wouldn't make the fight fair, now would it?" Xavier tilted his head at him and glanced at the other men in the room. "We'd have to hold back. If it's to be a fair fight, we can't do that. We won't make ourselves lesser to please anyone here. Look, we're on the same side here, but we're not here to kiss ass and make friends. There are more important things to deal with right now than stroking egos. We don't need to fight to know who the winner is, and that's just how things are. It's no disrespect to any of you. Werewolves have spent decades hiding who they are so they can blend in, and we won't anymore. We might not be human, but we're people, too. We feel love and hate like all of you. Good and bad exist in our race just like yours. We might have our differences, but a lot is also the same." Xavier glared at Jack. "We aren't monsters, and none of you can force us to be something we're not. What we are is different, and the last time I checked, that's fine." Xavier exhaled heavily as his eyes wandered back to Alonzo.

Surprisingly, he grinned. "I agree. The vampires are the monsters here." He held his hand out to Xavier. "I'd rather have a wolf fighting beside me any day."

Xavier shook his hand.

Jack sucked his teeth as he walked past us. "You're a fucking sellout," he told Alonzo.

Alonzo didn't look fazed in the least.

A few other soldiers left with Jack, but many stayed behind. A few continued with their workout, while some walked over to us, introducing themselves.

I stepped away from the group as Natalie's eyes turned white.

She told them her eyes were white because she was an Enchanted, and the soldiers appeared interested in learning more.

I smiled. If this was what the world would become after this ended, it was a world I couldn't wait to see.

CHAPTER NINE
NATALIE

The vision I'd just had faded, and I swallowed the lump forming in my throat. I blinked rapidly, the fog before my eyes clearing, but they immediately started to burn with impending tears. I squeezed them shut to hold the tears back as I reached out and placed my hand on the cool wall for support. Sometimes, being able to see into the future was more of a burden than a gift.

I opened my eyes and inhaled deeply before continuing down the hall. For two days, I'd enjoyed having Ruby and Xavier back. While everyone had been busy, it'd been nice just being able to see each other. My vision made it clear that would be ending soon.

"Natalie?" I turned around.

General Presley was just stepping out of a room. He closed the door softly and walked over to me. "It's pretty late. Are you okay?"

"Ah, yeah, I was just going to Ruby's room," I told him, my nails digging into my palm behind my back.

I was not sure when it happened or how, but there had been this connection between Presley and me ever since I got here. He wasn't my mate, but I definitely felt attracted to him. I'd never been crazy about finding a mate. While I'd found human men attractive before, I'd never dated any seriously or had strong feelings for any of them. I've never had strong feelings for any man, wolf or human; relationships had never been my thing.

However, something about Presley always made me smile when I saw him. The first time we met, after he had discovered our camp and wanted to take Ruby, there had been no time to find him attractive. Then I mind linked with him asking for his help, and he came through. I guess something about being in each others' minds built a greater level of intimacy between us. I'd noticed our eyes locking with each other quite a bit since then. When he was around, it felt like the chemistry between us was palpable.

He carried himself so well, and while he was intense at times, I liked it.

"Oh," he drawled as he looked down for a second. "And here I thought you were looking for me."

I arched a brow at this.

He closed his eyes. "Sorry." He chuckled. "That sounded so much better in my head."

"Less cheesy?" I asked with a chuckle.

"Way less."

I turned to walk away. "So, do you ever sleep, or are you always working?"

He stepped in stride next to me. "Always working," he replied with a smile. "Wanna know what my secret is?"

I nodded.

He exhaled heavily as if he was about to drop a bomb on me. "I'm a robot." He continued walking, his face showing no signs of him joking.

"You're not serious, are you?"

He stopped and turned to me slowly.

I looked him up and down, my eyes narrowing somewhat.

Suddenly, he started laughing. "I'm not a robot, Natalie. Seriously, relax."

To my surprise, a dimple on his left cheek popped out. Shaking my head, I stalked off. "Ha-ha-ha, laugh it up."

"I can't believe you actually fell for that," he chuckled as he caught up to me.

I shrugged. "I'm a werewolf, remember? I bet most people would believe you were a robot before they'd believe I was a werewolf. As a government operative, I am sure I don't have to tell you that Artificial Intelligence has come a long way. Hell, who knows what government technology is really capable of?"

He puckered his mouth, a look of contemplation on his face. "You're right. My outlook on many things needs to change now that I know there are people like you in the world. There is so much we humans don't know."

"You have no idea," I muttered under my breath as I exhaled.

"Hey..." He touched my elbow lightly. "Are you okay? You look a little pale."

I halted to look up at him and gave him a tight-lipped smile. "I'm okay, I'm just... I feel like I'm barely needed around here. I mean, when this all started, I was helping to protect Ruby. Now, she's the one who'll protect us all. Xavier, Axel, and Mathieu have been busy training with your men, and me..." I shrugged. "I'm just here, the girl with the visions. I wish..." I stopped talking as two soldiers, a man and woman, walked by us.

They both looked at us as if we were committing a crime.

Presley turned to them, his lips parting to say something.

I placed my hand on his arm. "Don't," I stopped him. "It's not worth it."

"I'm sorry. A lot of the people here are..." He sighed. "Not everyone has graciously accepted the revelation that supernaturals are real. You guys are stronger, faster, more powerful beings, and they feel threatened. To be completely honest, with vampires murdering everyone, they are terrified of all supernaturals."

I shook my head as I bit my lip. "I know they are, but you don't need to be sorry, Presley. You're not them, and I can never thank you enough for what you did for my pack. I'm going to check on Ruby, okay? I need to speak with her."

He stepped back with a nod. "Of course."

I smiled at him and moved away.

"Natalie?"

I looked back at him.

He buried his hands in his pockets. "There is no one else like you in the world, and you are needed. Please always remember that. You saved your pack when you contacted me."

The look in his blue eyes had my chest tightening, and I swallowed hard.

A few seconds passed with us just standing there and staring at each other. Sharing this moment with him was making me sad, because I knew nothing could ever or would ever happen between us.

"Thanks." I smiled and turned away, the burning behind my eyes returning. There were things I needed to tell the others before they left. I just had to figure out how to explain that I could have stopped so many things from happening.

⎯⎯⎯•◦ ◦•⎯⎯⎯

RUBY

The room I was given was more like a broom closet, but nothing I wasn't used to. For the past few months, I'd been dealing with worse, anyway. The tiny bed against the wall was surprisingly comfortable, but still, I couldn't sleep.

One of Presley's teams in the field was killed by vampires, so the Queen's attack was delayed. Fortunately, it gave Xavier and Axel time to work with Presley's men, so they could become familiar with working alongside humans and vice versa. Tensions weren't as high as they were when we initially arrived. Even though

I still got the odd curious or hateful stare, I felt less bothered by them.

Anyone who didn't like me could just kiss my ass for all I cared. Whether they liked me or not, I had a job to do here. I was going to kill the vampire Queen and make sure the rest of the world survived, no matter what anyone else thought of me.

I groaned and rolled to my side. That was partly why I couldn't sleep. I saw the way the humans who actually wanted to work with us looked at me, as if I was a celebrity or some kind of savior. I'd never experienced any of this before, especially being looked at with love and admiration.

I turned onto my stomach and stared at my door. When did I start referring to humans as such, as if I wasn't one of them? I closed my eyes and sighed, but I opened them a second later as my door opened.

"Why aren't you sleeping?" Natalie asked me as she walked in and closed the door behind her.

Sitting up and folding my legs lotus-style, I made space for her to sit beside me. "I could ask you the same thing."

She held her head back against the wall and sighed. "I can't sleep."

"Same," I grumbled. "What's on your mind?"

She quirked her mouth a bit before turning her head to look at me. She exhaled heavily. "I've just been thinking about when you guys leave to kill the Queen."

"If it *is* the Queen," I interjected.

She shrugged. "If it's her or not, I've just been thinking about when you guys leave."

"Are you worried that we won't come back?" I asked her.

Looking away, Natalie blinked slowly. I noticed her eyes looked puffy as if she'd been crying.

I nudged her with my elbow. "Whether it's the Queen or not, we're all coming back."

She turned her gaze to me. "I know you all will," she said softly before smiling. "Are you scared?"

I combed my hair back and out of my face. "I'm terrified. I feel like everything is just beginning and ending at the same time. What if it is the Queen?"

"Then you kill her," she answered matter-of-factly.

I snorted. "I don't even know how," I mumbled.

She placed her hand over mine. "When the time comes, you will."

My eyes roamed her face for a moment. "How do you know that?"

She shrugged. "I just do. The Goddess wouldn't have picked you if she didn't believe you could do what needs to be done. Plus..." She tilted her head towards me as she looked at me from under her lashes. "You aren't fighting this alone. Hell, you've got two hot Alphas out there backing you up, not to mention the best soldiers the U.S. government has to offer."

I smiled and nodded.

We both sat in silence for a moment.

"So, you and Presley," I broke the quiet.

Her head snapped towards me in surprise.

I chuckled. "Come on, it's obvious. So, what's going on with you two?"

She smiled and shook her head. "Nothing right now. I think he likes me, though."

"Do you like him?"

She nodded, and the smile on her lips faded.

I could see something was bothering her.

"I do like him, but nothing will ever happen between us."

"You don't know that, Natalie. I mean, I know you're not big on finding your mate anyways. Just remember, with the way things are going right now, it's important to tell people how you feel."

Staring down at her hands, she turned a bead ring around and around her finger. "Yeah, you're right." She turned to face me and pulled me into a hug. "I'm so glad we became friends. You are the sister I never had."

I was frozen for a moment, a bit confused, but then I hugged her back. I pouted as I became emotional and squeezed her closer. "I'm glad too. And I feel the same way about you. In fact, I hate everyone but you."

Chuckling, she pulled away. "I think there might be at least two more people you don't hate around here. You should take your own advice, you know. Talk to the guys about how you feel about them."

I bit at my lip to hide the smile growing on my lips.

She narrowed her eyes at me as she looked me up and down. "What? Ruby, you better tell me."

"I kissed them," I whispered.

Her eyes widened.

"Yup, I kissed them both, and we kind of all slept together."

Her mouth dropped as her eyes widened further.

"Hey, get your mind out of the gutter! Nothing happened!" I exclaimed.

She pinned me with a look that said she didn't believe me.

"I swear, nothing happened. We just slept together in the same bed. It was after I found out Malcolm was my dad and everything about Lovette being my mom. I... needed them. I needed them both."

"Wow," she exclaimed in astonishment. "So, things are better between you and Axel?"

I nodded. "Things are better. I think we'll both always remember what happened, but I've learned so much about him, and him about me. With becoming..." I gestured down my body. "...this, and all the emotions and everything happening, Xavier and I have had our moments when we've felt far from each other, but... I know I can count on them both."

"So you guys are legit going to go along with this crazy throuple?" she asked with a wide grin.

My face started to burn with a blush as I nodded. "I mean, I don't want either of them to reject me, and I don't think either of them wants to reject me, either. So..." I inhaled and exhaled deeply, the heat in my cheeks transferring to the rest of my body. "I guess this is how things will be between us."

"I've missed out on a lot." She sighed, despite the pleased look on her face. "Today, I saw them both laughing together. It was like watching a unicorn peeing."

I made a face. "I don't even know what—wait." I squinted at her. "Are unicorns real?"

Natalie busted out laughing. "Hell, no."

"Oh," I said with a laugh. "Well, Xavier and Axel have their moments." I rubbed my eyes. "And in other news, I... um, I spoke to her. My mom, I mean."

"I know. Xavier told me," she replied softly, a look of concern growing in her eyes. "He told me she's the one who took your memories and power."

Her expression made me want to cry. I nodded, my throat suddenly becoming dry. "I wish I could see her again."

"You won't see her again, not like before."

I frowned. "What do you mean?"

"The Goddess won't allow it. You'll see her again after you die, but you can't let that happen."

"Damn," I drawled as I unfolded my legs for them to dangle off the bed. "Harsh."

"Sorry."

"How do you know what the Goddess will or will not do?"

A knock came at the door, then it opened, revealing Presley on the other side. "I sent another team in. You need to see this."

⸺•◦ ◦•⸺

RUBY

The room filled with soldiers remained quiet. No one was typing away at the many keyboards or walking around in a rush. Everyone seemed focused on the large television on the wall, showing a somewhat shaky body cam video of humans being removed from two trucks and being led into the same building the vampire Queen was observed entering.

My stomach clenched as children were led out of the truck as well.

Being that it was nighttime and in the forest, the only light came from the moon and two large lights above the building's front door.

"That's a General." Xavier pointed to the screen as another car pulled up to the house, and a man headed over to it.

"How do you know?" Presley asked.

Axel stepped forward, his arms crossed over his broad chest. "We encountered one before. It looks like this vampire is wearing a full red uniform with black lines down his arms—the same uniform as the one we saw earlier. "

My blind ass hadn't been able to make that out with the General we had met. Now, however, I could see it with the subtle lighting. We watched the man on the screen walk towards the car to open the passenger's door. A woman stepped out of the car. All that could be seen was the top of her head a second before she was immediately flanked by the guards, who appeared to be wearing black uniforms with red lines. They walked closely by her as they led her into the building, and the door closed behind them.

"We can't tell if it's even the same woman as before," I told the others as I looked away from the screen.

Everyone in the command room filed out, heading back to their assigned tasks.

"The humans... all those humans are also our priority," Presley replied. "We leave in an hour."

"What?" I asked as I spun around to face him. "An hour?"

"Yes, Ruby." Presley's brows knitted. "If we wait any longer, all those humans will be killed."

I looked back at the now-frozen screen and swallowed the lump that had lodged in my throat. Yes, we needed to save all those humans, but I hoped I'd have more time before facing the Queen. "You said you had ways to help me with my power. Yet I've been here for two full days, and I've only been training with the guys," I told him as I turned to face him.

"We had a way of helping you—a person, to be exact—but our asset was lost. Now that I know what you are and what you're capable of, my help wouldn't have been much help at all. Are you ready for this, Ruby? We have to act now, or all those—"

"I know," I interjected, cutting him off. I clenched my fists at my sides as I pictured the children I had seen in the video. "I'm ready."

Presley nodded his head sternly, his eyes drifting to Natalie briefly. "We move out in an hour." He then turned to a soldier. "Get them ready."

The soldier saluted him. "Yes, General."

Presley moved away.

I immediately turned to Natalie. I shook my head at her as my heart hammered in my chest as if it was trying to break free. "I'm not ready."

"We'll be there with you," Axel tried to comfort me.

I looked his way.

His hazel eyes drifted to Xavier.

Xavier nodded in agreement. "If that was the Queen, we might not get another chance like this," he added. "We've got this."

I chewed on my bottom lip and released my clenched fists. "Okay," I exhaled. "It's now or never, I guess."

I stepped closer to the television as the video started playing again.

THE VAMPIRE GENERAL

I closed my eyes and inhaled, and it was as if I could still smell her. I finally understood why Bleeders who had come into contact with her became so bloodthirsty.

I saw why the Queen was so interested in her. Ruby Saunders was not of this earth; I could smell it in her blood. The memory of her killing those Bleeders jumped to the forefront of my mind, and I opened my eyes. I was staring up at the ceiling with my head held back on the sofa, but what I was actually seeing was her sucking the life from those Bleeders.

The Queen had said there hadn't been someone like her in a long time, but I suspected there had never been anyone like her. We decided to enact our plans now because the earth's creatures—both human and otherwise—had grown so far away from the Gods. The fewer who worshipped the gods, the further they fell out of the gods' favor. Creatures of the earth had more power centuries ago. The poor fools had no idea how far they had fallen. Not only that, species no longer allied with each other. They were too busy keeping to themselves and hiding from humans.

Sadly, we had miscalculated the weakness of our greatest enemies. As divided as the werewolves had been, they still held their Goddess close—much closer than we knew. The bitch even left one of her children to thwart our efforts.

I wanted to see what the whelp was capable of. I wanted to see who this girl was that my Queen both feared and desired to have as her own. I saw now that she had reason to. I smiled as I looked to the ground at the two humans lying there, their eyes lifeless and dull. I could also see how much more powerful we'd become if she became one of us.

A supernatural who was turned became full vampire, not a hybrid. They became as bloodthirsty as the rest of us and turned into a Bleeder or a Skin. Yet, this Ruby had the blood of a goddess running through her, so what would happen if she turned? When

I asked the Queen, she merely grinned like a Cheshire cat and assured me Ruby would become "a very powerful ally" for us.

A knock came at the door.

"Come in," I said softly.

The door opened as a female vampire with a severely humped back and sagging, wrinkled skin slowly walked in. She was one of the Queen's Seers, and one of three Enchanteds the Queen had turned over the years. All three women were extremely powerful and very old vampires who had retained their ability to see into the future.

It finally clicked, and I couldn't believe I hadn't seen it before.

That was why the Queen wanted Ruby. If an Enchanted with diluted divinity could become so powerful from the turn, what would happen with someone like Ruby, with her raw divinity?

"The Queen would like to speak with you," the woman said in an eerie voice, her completely black eyes unreadable for even me.

I said nothing as I sat forward.

The Seer closed her eyes. She inhaled deeply like someone about to dive into water and she slowly started to stand straight. A bone in her back cracked, and as she stood upright, her black eyes turned red. "General Carden," the Seer greeted me. I could hear the queen's voice mingled with her voice. She looked at the bodies on the floor. "Relaxing, I see."

"No, my Queen, I'm planning for the upcoming attack," I confirmed.

The Seer walked over to the bodies and bent down. She moved the hair out of the woman's face before standing once more. "Where is she?"

I stood from the sofa. "I have my eyes on her. She's with the humans, my Queen."

"Then why haven't you taken her, Carden? I'm running out of patience," she asked through clenched teeth. "Olcan gave you her location before she found the humans. Why didn't you take her then?"

"I wanted to see what she was capable of, and I also wanted to see into her mind," I replied.

Even though I wasn't literally in the Queen's presence, the Seer's eyes were now her eyes. They instilled the same fear as if I were looking at the Queen herself.

After a moment, she rolled her hands in a circle, as if telling me to hurry up. "Okay, and what? What did you see?"

"Not much before she felt me inside her mind and blocked me, but I did see a memory. I saw William."

Her hand shot out and grabbed me around my throat.

I could feel blood running down my neck from where her nails had pierced my skin.

Stepping closer, she pulled me down to stare into her eyes. "Never say that name," she hissed before looking down at my throat. She released me slowly and sighed. "That better not be all you have to tell me." She arched a brow as she licked my blood from one of her fingers as she turned away.

"No, my Queen," I replied promptly. "The werewolf confirmed they were on their way to a human army base."

She turned her head but didn't look around. "Mm... well, you know what to do then, don't you?"

"Yes, my Queen," I replied obediently.

Now, the Seer's shoulders began to slump as she bent forward into her position before.

"Wait," I said.

The Seer turned to look at me, the red eyes of the Queen fading.

"My brother... has his body been retrieved?"

"Yes," she replied. "Those vermin killed your brother; they killed my son. Humans are the pests of this earth, never forget that. I want that base destroyed, do you understand?" She turned back around and stepped from the room slowly.

I clenched my teeth at the annoying tingling sensation of the wounds on my neck healing.

CHAPTER TEN
RUBY

Axel and Xavier were given earpieces to speak with everyone else if needed, along with the other werewolves that volunteered to come with us. There was no point in giving them guns or any of the other gadgets the humans had strapped to their bodies. They'd just be ripped to pieces when they transformed. Of course, with their heightened hearing, they really only needed the earpieces for the teams that would be too far away from us.

I was given one as well, along with a gun. I stared down at it in my palm and moved my hand up and down as I felt its weight. It seemed kind of silly for me to have a gun when my powers were more potent than any bullet, but Presley thought I should have one just in case.

"It has UV bullets," Alonzo clarified as he secured his bulletproof vest.

"Okay," I replied. "Why the vests, though?"

"The vampires obviously won't be using guns, but our gear gives us a little cushion when they attack us. You have your powers to rely on, Ruby, but keeping that gun on you won't hurt. It works great against the Bleeders."

"What about the Skins?"

"It works on them too, but while one bullet can kill a Bleeder, it takes a bit more than one for the Skins," he explained. "When this all happened, it took a while for the military to make a weapon that could kill them. The Bleeders can be killed easily, but the others..."

"Yeah, I know. Do you know if anyone has ever faced a General?" I asked him.

He sat down on top of a trunk filled with guns. "Well..." He looked around us before leaning forward. "I heard some of the higher-ranking officers talking. A General was killed in Paris."

I stepped closer to him. "Really? How?"

He shrugged. "I'm not sure how, but he killed sixty people before they could kill him."

My eyes widened for a second. "Jesus."

"Mmhmm, and get this: apparently, the Generals have special abilities. The one they killed in Paris could move things with his mind." He shook his head. "As if they weren't hard enough to kill as it was."

I realized that back at Olcan's place when we had been attacked, Olcan had said the Queen had already lost one of her Generals. None of us had even bothered to ask him how he knew that. But this explained why I could feel the General we had met in my mind.

Another soldier called Alonzo, and he walked away.

However, I remained there as I wondered what power the General we had seen in the video had. I placed a hand on the gun strapped to my side when Natalie appeared beside me.

"We need to talk," she told me, her face pale as she grabbed my hand and pulled me away from the others. "Now."

I allowed her to drag me to the corner of the room. "Um, yeah, sure, what's wrong?"

"I'm not going to beat around the bush, so I'm just going to rip the Band-Aid off," she whispered. "This is harder than you think."

My brows dipped at her now-panicked state. I placed my hand on her shoulder and shook her gently for her to look at me and stop looking at the others so wide-eyed. "Natalie, you're freaking me out. What's going on?"

"I knew you were going to be attacked," she said, her words coming out in a rush.

My nose wrinkled as I smelled blood. I looked down to see that she was sinking one of her claws into the palm of her hand. My hand fell from her shoulder as I stepped back.

Sighing, she released her hand. She looked relieved as she clenched her fist.

"What?" I asked, my voice low. "Which time?"

She stared at me from under her lashes, a look of regret in her eyes. "The first time you were bitten by a vampire, when you, Xavier, and Axel ran from Olcan."

I started blinking rapidly, not sure if I was hearing her correctly. "I'm sorry." I held my hand up. "What are you talking about?"

Sighing, she combed her white hair backward. "I saw a vision of you being attacked before you left."

My stomach twisted with anger and confusion.

Natalie stepped forward, her words coming out rushed, "I couldn't say anything. I swear. I wish I had been able to, but the Goddess wouldn't let me."

I stared at her for a moment, unable to speak.

She visibly swallowed as she waited for me to say something.

I couldn't formulate the words. I was upset she had allowed that to happen to me, she had been the one to encourage Xavier and me to leave, and all along, she had known we would be attacked and almost killed. "Did you know Malcolm would be there?" I asked softly.

"What?"

"The person that saved us that night, it turns out it was Malcolm. Did you know he would be there to save me?"

She looked away.

I shook my head as I clenched my fists at my sides. "You didn't know if I was going to live or die, and yet, you helped it to happen by offering to facilitate our escape from Olcan?"

"The Goddess wouldn't have let you die." She moved closer to me.

I raised my head. I knew in my agitated state that my eyes were shifting from black to green and back.

With a gasp, Natalie stepped back.

"You've been working with her all this time?" I demanded. "How much have you known, Natalie? What other secrets are you hiding? You could have warned us all about the vampires. You could have given us all a head start on defeating them. We could have stopped all of this."

"Nothing could have stopped them at that point, Ruby. I wanted to tell you, I swear I did, but I literally *couldn't* say anything. The Goddess forbade it."

"Well, how are you telling me now? Huh?" I asked her.

She sighed heavily.

I couldn't believe her. I felt like I didn't know her at all. The Natalie I knew, or I *thought* I knew, wouldn't have kept something like this a secret. I turned away from her.

Sure enough, Xavier and Axel were looking our way. From the angry look on their faces, they heard our conversation.

"Ruby, please, you have to believe me. I wanted to tell you, but I couldn't... I'm sorry," Natalie pleaded.

I kept moving away from her. She was the very first person I learned to trust after falling into this world, and now she was telling me she knew all along about The Goddess's plans for me. "Did you know everything? Did you know about my mom and Malcolm?"

"No, she didn't tell me anything other than war was coming

and you'd play a major part in it. She wanted me to stay by you and help guide you, but that's all I knew. I swear."

"Guide me, huh?" I glanced at Xavier and Axel. "Is no one in my life there without a purpose to serve for the Goddess?"

"Let's go, everyone, time to move out!" Presley yelled as he entered the room. He looked at Xavier and Axel, and then followed their stares to Natalie and me. He frowned as he stared at Natalie and then at me. Remaining silent, he walked off purposefully.

"Why are you telling me this now?" I asked her.

She stared at me, the rim of her eyes red with tears. "It's time you knew. I know you're angry at me. You have every right to be, but no matter how hard or painful some things that happen are, they can't be stopped. If something is meant to happen, it will."

I had no doubt my eyes were rimmed with tears too, as I snorted and turned away.

"Ruby?"

I stopped but didn't turn around.

"I'm truly sorry," she apologized.

I clenched my fists as I walked past the guys, then stopped at the door.

Natalie told Xavier and Axel goodbye.

Xavier replied, "We'll talk when I get back."

"I love you, and I am sorry," she apologized as she embraced him.

I closed my eyes at the pain in her voice, but I felt too angry to look at her.

That night, I had been so terrified and confused. I thought I was going to die, and she knew it would happen. I thought Natalie was my friend, the only true friend I've ever had. Apparently I'd been very wrong. Did she approach me that day in the library because the Goddess told her to? Or did the Goddess make her do it without her even knowing?

I pulled my hair into a high ponytail and then made a bun.

Fuck the Goddess.

I was so goddamn sick of her intervention in every aspect of my life, from my birth to my mates, and now even my friends. My life had been nothing but heartache and pain thanks to her. Now I was off to kill a vampire Queen with no clue how I would even do it. The Goddess had used everyone in my life to shepard me to this point. Could I even rightfully call it *my* life?

I stepped outside.

Presley, who had been waiting, led me to one of six helicopters.

My rage was only continuing to steadily grow as I got into the helicopter.

Presley helped to strap me in and kept sending odd looks my way. When Axel and Xavier joined us, they both sent me looks of concern.

I avoided looking at them all and closed my eyes as the helicopter lifted off the ground.

The sooner this all ended, the sooner I could vanish and have nothing to do with Gods, or anyone who expected something from me for that matter. I'd grown tired of everyone looking to me to bring an end to this war.

I felt so tired of all of this.

My eyes were stinging with tears, but I kept them closed as I squeezed the straps around my body. If I looked at Xavier or Axel, I would break down, and right now, I needed the anger coursing through my veins.

I needed my rage to do what had to be done.

———— •• ••• ————

RUBY

I wasn't sure how much time had passed since we left the base. This was my first time flying in a helicopter, but my mind was too crammed with thoughts to focus on the experience. My gaze remained glued outside at the blue sky and white clouds.

Natalie's words had been replaying in my mind since we'd left. She had known what would happen to me, and even if she hadn't known everything about who or what I was, she knew enough that we could've gotten in front of this mess earlier. I didn't buy her crap about The Goddess not allowing her to tell. She just told me now with no apparent objections from the Goddess.

How had she been able to look me in the face all this time? That night had been one of the worst experiences of my life.

Sighing, I looked towards the guys and found them speaking to each other, but since I wasn't wearing a headset, I couldn't hear them. Axel's hazel eyes drifted to me, and the knowing look he gave me, one of pity, made me look away. I didn't want anyone's pity.

Both he and Xavier were a part of the Goddess's plans too. She did this. She made it so I would be a mate to them both. I still didn't understand the reason for that, but everyone in my life had been placed there by her like little chess pieces on a lifesize gameboard.

I grew up an orphan. I had no one to love or love me back, no responsibility but to survive and care for myself. Suddenly, I was supposed to put that all aside and save the world. I could think of a lot of better ways I could have been groomed for this.

Presley tapped my leg.

I looked to the side.

He pointed downwards that we were about to land.

I nodded. Holding onto the straps across my chest, I clenched my jaw as the helicopter started to descend.

Once on the ground, Presley helped me to make my way out of the helicopter, and I realized we had landed alone.

"Where are the others?" I asked as I glanced at the other seven men who had flown with us.

"Circling the perimeter; we can't afford for the Queen to escape. There are werewolves with each team, so hopefully, that'll give us an advantage. Our team will be going in through the front door."

"Oh." I turned in a circle. The forest seemed so quiet, unnaturally so. "There's something wrong with this place. I can feel it."

"Are you okay?" Axel whispered to my ear.

I looked his way. I knew he wasn't asking me about what I was feeling right now. He was asking about what had happened with Natalie.

I nodded. "I'm fine, I'm just nervous. You're all putting too much faith in a novice."

"We're putting our faith in someone that has proven she can do what no one else can," Presley replied. "We're all new to this threat, Ruby; we're all just novices trying to survive."

"Team three in location," a voice reported over the earpiece we all had.

Presley replied that they would wait for all the teams to get into position. "We need to use up the sun while we have it, guys. The vampires can't and won't try to escape while the sun's out. We need to act now," he announced. "Even with the sun on our side and the element of surprise, stay on guard. We could all still be slaughtered."

Five minutes passed before all teams reported that they had landed and were in position. Presley quietly led us through the forest with Axel by his side up front to lend a listening ear to the forest while Xavier stayed at our rear. I walked in the middle with the other soldiers.

The closer we got to the vampires' hideout, the more I feared they might hear my hammering heartbeat and know we were coming.

This is it.

I felt like throwing up. At the same time, I was eager to see this war come to an end.

The smell of vampires hit me like a ton of bricks, and I had to hold back from coughing.

Ahead of us, Axel held his hand up for everyone to stop. He then whispered to Presley, who then gave hand signals to his men.

I watched as they all grabbed their guns and began fanning out somewhat.

Xavier came up beside me and held my hand. He squeezed it gently before raising it to his lips. I sighed as some of the tension in my body left as he mouthed to me, *"I'm here."*

I needed to remember I wasn't doing this entirely alone.

Presley called us forward to the tree line where we bent down to stare at the house a few yards away. The three-story building was run-down with blacked-out windows. The massive parking lot in front of it made for the perfect ground for what we planned. We heard no sounds, no birds or insects, and the wind around us went still. The vampires' scent was so strong, my eyes began to water. There was most definitely a lot of them here.

I think the Bleeders were the ones with a more pungent scent. When I killed that vampire so long ago, a Skin, he had a vampire's scent, but it wasn't as horrible as the Bleeders.

"Move in," Presley directed through his mic, and all guns were aimed as his men started moving stealthily forward, breaking through the tree line. He looked at me. "Are you ready?"

I nodded as I called on my power, allowing all of it to flow through me like a river. "It's now or never," I replied.

He tilted his head towards the house, and we moved forward as well.

Xavier walked in front of me, with Axel at my back alongside General Presley.

I looked past Xavier to see another team breaking through the tree line as well on the other side of the parking lot. I noted the three werewolves along them were already in their wolf form.

"Wait," Axel suddenly commanded, and we stopped.

"What?" Presley whispered back, a look of annoyance on his face.

Axel's eyes changed to black as he looked around us. "Something's wrong," he said ominously.

Yeah, no shit. This place is beyond creepy.

"We can't hear anything," Axel stated the obvious.

"Yeah, so?" Xavier asked.

Axel shook his head. "It shouldn't be this quiet, even in the daytime. You and I should be able to hear them, at least one of them. There's nothing," Axel replied, his fangs and nails elongating as he spoke. "It's daytime, but not all of them would be sleeping. Wouldn't they have guards awake?"

I spun around to look at Presley, who was now looking around us as well. My body jolted as thunder clapped above us, and we all looked up as the beautiful blue sky started to change. Black storm clouds rolled in.

I looked over at Xavier with panicked eyes. "Does that seem unnatural to anyone else, or is it just me?"

Xavier started to remove his shirt, and so did Axel.

A lightning bolt struck the ground in the parking lot, the world around us dark as if it was evening, going on to nighttime.

The front door to the house opened and a man stepped out. The red uniform with black was unmistakable.

Axel's wolf by my side looked at me.

I clenched my fists as I looked back at the General.

The vamps knew we were coming.

"He's doing this," Xavier said in a strained voice as he fell to the ground, the brown fur of his wolf bursting through his skin. "Look at his... eyes."

Sure enough, the vampire's eyes were a pure white instead of the typical crimson. His hair which stopped just above his ears was a matching shade of white. With his pale skin, his overall features combined to form an exotic look I would've never associated with a vampire. That was, until he looked directly at me and smiled, revealing razor-sharp fangs. Those were familiar, at least.

The sound of the breaking ground came from behind us, and we spun around to see a Bleeder digging its way from out of the ground.

Presley fired at it straightaway. The bullet lodged itself between the creature's eyes, and it fell dead.

Lightning struck the ground again. With each flash, more Bleeders began to appear from beneath us.

With the sun blocked out, we'd lost one of our biggest advantages.

Presley yelled out orders and gunshots started to echo all around us.

Axel jumped into the air and tackled a vampire making its way towards us.

Xavier remained by my side, his head low and his legs wide apart as he readied himself for an attack.

I reached out and placed my hand on Xavier's side. I closed my eyes as I inhaled deeply. The sound of wolves growling and snarling mixed with resounding gunshots, and the chilling hisses of the vampires filled my head. I tried to clear my mind as I gathered as much energy from the earth as I could pull.

Without opening my eyes, I sensed a Bleeder making its way towards Xavier. I held my hand out, releasing the energy I had absorbed.

I opened my eyes in time to see the Bleeder flying backward as if he'd been thrown, along with another two behind it.

The werewolves ripped into two of them while Presley shot the other. Thunder rumbled over us. Lightning struck just in front of Xavier and me, sending us flying backward.

I looked up in time to see the sky open as another lightning bolt started to descend to the earth. Using my mind, I pushed Xavier's wolf out of the way just in time, and the bolt struck the ground where he had been lying just moments before.

He got to his feet and shook his head but was tackled by a Bleeder.

"Hello, Ruby," a voice said from behind me.

I turned around.

The General slapped me across the face, sending me skidding across the ground. "Oh, I'm sorry. The Queen wants you alive. I forgot for a second there."

Easing myself up on my hands, I got up slowly, a cut on my arm already healing. "She's not here, is she?"

He chuckled. "Of course not. Did you all really think we wouldn't know men were watching us? Oh, I'm Alaris, by the way."

I don't give a shit what this monster's name is! As I got to my feet, I clenched my teeth as my body started to grow hot. I focused on channeling it all into my hands.

The vampire vanished from my sight. One moment he was standing there, a sinister smile on his pale face, and then he was gone.

This asshole is mocking me. He's toying with me, but if I can't even handle him, how will I ever face the Queen?

"Now, I'd prefer it if you didn't try to burn me," Alaris whispered from behind me.

I spun around, releasing the built-up heat in my hands, but it caught a Bleeder instead of my intended target.

"Wow," he said from my left as he watched the Bleeder turn to ash on the ground. "I'm impressed, but also very disappointed. Are you really the girl my mother fears?"

His mother?

A soldier ran up beside me and began emptying his clip into Alaris. I watched as he yelped in pain as his body was knocked backward with each bullet that entered him. He vanished before our eyes. Suddenly, the soldier by my side was yanked away.

I watched Alaris break the soldier's neck and decapitate him with ease, as if he were nothing but a toy soldier instead of actual flesh and blood. My knees grew weak, and I felt utterly sick to my stomach.

I screamed, my body shaking with emotion, and the ground beneath us started to crack. Tree roots appeared from beneath us, lashing out at Alaris and striking anyone close enough.

All of this death and killing; none of this is right!

Lightning hit the ground beside me, sending me flying and falling onto a Bleeder who instantly tried to bite me. I grabbed its face and threw it off me with more force than I knew I was capable of.

"Well, well, now you're showing your true colors, Ms. Saunders," Alaris teased.

I got to my feet as he approached me slowly. I watched as the holes in his chest started to heal.

He dove as roots from the earth lashed out at him, but he stood in front of me within the next second.

"Where is she?" I yelled at him.

He smiled. "Come with me, and I'll take you to her. There won't be anything or anyone left alive here or back at your base, anyway."

My face fell. "What did you say?"

A werewolf suddenly tackled him to the ground, and a Skin attacked me. I hadn't even realized there were a few of them among the Bleeders.

"You smell amazing," the man hissed as we struggled on the ground.

Kicking him in the side, I flipped us over and grabbed his throat. "You don't!" Black veins appeared on my arms, and he physically caught fire beneath me. I got off him, my heart now pounding with panic at what Alaris had said. I looked around at the bodies on the ground and those still fighting before I spotted Alaris with his fangs in a werewolf's throat.

The smell of blood was strong in the air, mixed with the

pungent odor of the vampires. I walked forward slowly, my eyes trained on the General.

He looked my way and stood up, wiping his hand across his mouth.

"What have you done?" I demanded. Despite the distance between us, I knew he could hear me just fine.

He held his palm out as a lightning bolt began to dance within his palm. "While all your forces are here, many of ours are at your army base. There will be no one left alive."

For a second, I couldn't breathe as Natalie's blue eyes flashed within my mind. It felt as if a hand were holding my lungs and squeezing them. "No," I said under my breath.

The roots still protruding from the ground started to move erratically as I lost control of my powers. Natalie, Mathieu, and all the others were in danger. This wasn't just a trap for us.

The sadness in Natalie's eyes before we had left was all I could see. As angry as I was with her, I had every intention of going back and talking things over. *What if she's—*

I didn't finish the thought as my face burned with rage.

Alaris held his hand up to the sky. A bolt of lightning fell into his palm, and he threw it at me.

I couldn't move, and I didn't blink as it came to me. I merely closed my eyes.

The impact rocked my body, but I remained standing as I absorbed the bolt. It was pure, raw energy, and I could feel the hairs on my body standing on end. As I opened my eyes, I sent the bolt rolling back towards him.

It burned through his chest, its power tripled by mine. He rolled onto his side as he gripped at his chest and reached up to the sky with his other hand.

Thunder rumbled above us as three bolts broke through the clouds.

I bit down on my lip until I tasted blood and reached out with both hands. Energy—it was all energy. I drank it into my body as if it was water and I hadn't had a drop in years.

The bolts changed their position, all three bolts hitting me at once. I felt like an empty battery being charged as I consumed it all. I smiled as my body started to emit small bolts of lightning.

Bleeders and Skins alike were being killed, fried to a crisp, when suddenly someone barreled into me.

"You fucking bitch!" Alaris yelled as he climbed on top of me on the ground. He put his hand around my throat to cut my air off as he reached up to the sky with his other hand. "The Queen wants you alive, but she never said you had to be in one piece."

The cloud above us opened. A ray of sunlight broke through, killing a Skin as it ran into the light. Lightning struck, the bolt coming down onto Alaris and me.

I closed my eyes.

I thought of my mother's words, to stop fearing my power, to open myself. My hand holding Alaris's wrist reached out, and instead of the bolt falling into his hands, it hit him full force. The smell of his burning skin had my nose burning, and he released me to get away. Before he could get anywhere, I grabbed his face, pouring all the heat I could muster into his body before kicking him off me.

I held my hands up to the sky, commanding the clouds to move away, and they complied. Sunlight broke through the darkness around us, as did lightning. The screams and shrieks of vampires filled my ears, and I laughed maniacally as those screams grew louder.

Alaris himself turned to ash beneath my feet.

I heard someone yell my name, and I spun around. Presley was stooped down over a soldier on the ground, and I could see the large burn mark on the soldier's shoulder and neck.

My hands fell to my sides, and the lightning storm stopped.

All around, werewolves and soldiers were staring at me, some in awe, others in fear, and some visibly trembled.

I walked over to Presley slowly.

The soldier on the ground stared up at me with watery eyes.

"I'm so sorry." I fell to my knees beside him.

His chest, shoulders, and neck were badly burned.

I leaned over him, saddened to see the hurt and pain I had caused him from using my powers. This was precisely what I had feared, inadvertently hurting someone when I used my powers. Tears started rolling down my cheeks. Then something unexpected happened. As a tear from my eye landed on the soldier's shoulder, he started to heal. I placed my hand over him because I knew somehow, I could stop his pain. I tried to visualize absorbing all the injury and inflammation in his body into myself. His face went from a grimace of discomfort to one of relaxation.

"Thank you, Ruby," he whispered.

I squeezed his hand to acknowledge. I stood and walked to another wounded soldier on the ground, a deep burn on his chest.

He was gasping for breath, and I took the hand he weakly held out to me. I healed him as well, sadness welling up inside me. It seemed like for every good thing I'd done so far, I'd hurt someone in the process.

"We need to get back to the base right away," I told Presley as he appeared to my left. "They're attacking the base. We have to save Natalie and the others."

CHAPTER ELEVEN
RUBY

We spotted a cloud of black smoke a mile out from the base.

Xavier couldn't sit still, and before the helicopter even landed, he opened the door and jumped out.

Axel followed behind him.

I waited until the helicopter was at least on the ground before getting out and rushing towards the building.

Around us, there were dead bodies scattered on the ground, both humans and vampires.

"How did they attack during the day?" I asked out loud as I looked around me.

"Natalie! Dad!" Xavier yelled as he entered the building as Axel and I followed close behind.

Soldiers rushed in behind us, and the werewolves that had gone with us killed the vampires that still appeared to be alive but wounded.

"Fuck," Presley mumbled.

When I looked around, he was staring down at a female soldier on the ground who was writhing in pain, her arms and legs bent in odd directions.

"What's wrong with her?" I asked.

He pointed to the bite mark on her neck. "She's turning," he answered through clenched teeth and pulled out his gun.

I looked away.

Gunshots began to echo around us, and I tried to block out the fact that these soldiers were being forced to kill their colleagues and friends. How had the vampires done this? How had they attacked during the day? The dead vampires scattered around us couldn't have been the only ones who attacked the base, so where were the others?

I pushed those thoughts away for the meantime as I rushed around like everyone else, trying to spot a familiar head of white hair.

"Have you seen Natalie? She's the werewolf with white hair," I asked two men who passed by me carrying a dead vampire in their arms.

They shook their heads, and I kept moving. I felt so fatigued, my body spent from all the power I had used, but I needed to find her. I was running by the cafeteria when I looked inside and saw her. My heart dropped and shattered into a million pieces as I rushed inside. I fell to the ground beside her, ignoring the pain in my knees from the impact. "Natalie? Natalie, it's me, we're—oh, my god," I didn't know what to do, I didn't know where to look or where to heal first.

Her body was covered in bite marks, her blood creating a pool around her. I screamed for Xavier and Axel as I started to heal her wounds. She looked so pale, her blue eyes so dull. I tried to avoid looking at her face, or I'd lose concentration. Everything that I had been angry at her for was now irrelevant.

"Ruby?" she asked weakly.

I wiped my tears away, smearing her blood on my face in the process. "It's me, it's me. It's okay, I-I can help you. I can stop the bleeding." I wiped my face again and got up to move to her other side.

Axel rushed into the room.

I looked his way, his wide hazel eyes causing more tears to roll down my cheeks. "Help me," I choked out. "Help me, please! She's dying." Her hand wrapped around my wrist, and I looked down at her, a hot tear sliding down my cheek. "It's okay, just hang on, okay. Where the fuck is Xavier?"

"He found his dad. Mathieu's wounded," Axel replied.

"Ruby, stop," Natalie whispered.

I moved on from the bite on her wrist and placed my hand over the one on her shoulder.

"I said stop."

"I have to heal you!" I yelled at her, my frustration causing my hands to start shaking.

"I can feel it happening, Ruby." She closed her eyes for a second before opening them again. "I can feel the change happening. They didn't just drink from me this time."

I started crying as my hand fell away from her neck.

"I'm sorry I didn't tell you everything. I-I wanted to but—"

"None of that matters anymore, Natalie, there has to be something I can do. You can't become one of them!"

"This was meant to happen, Ruby. I told you before; what's meant to happen will." She started coughing.

Presley rushed into the room behind Axel. The color drained from his face as he rushed forward, but he stopped at where Natalie's blood had pooled on the ground.

"Listen," Natalie whispered.

I wiped her blood away from the corner of her mouth. Never before had I felt so utterly useless.

"You might feel as if your life is being played with, but it's not. You've been given a gift and the chance for your legacy to live on forever, Ruby. You'll never be forgotten, and everyone will know who you are, the woman that saved us all. I-I won't be here, but I'll die happy that I had the privilege of being your friend."

"Jesus, Natalie, stop, please, just stop!" I tried once more to heal the bite on her neck but she moved my hand away. "I can't do any of this without you, dammit! I don't know what I'm doing! Every time I think I have everything handled, I turn around and see that I've hurt someone. If—if I'm so powerful, why can't I save you? What good are my powers if they can't save you!"

"Not everyone can be saved, Ruby..." Her face twisted in pain. "Trust your powers," she added after a moment, "and a door will open for you."

She closed her eyes.

I panicked for a moment thinking she was gone, but her lips parted as she started chanting under her breath. I leaned forward, but it was a language I didn't understand. A wooden box suddenly appeared by my side, and she fell silent.

"Take it," she choked out, her hand slowly rising to grip at her throat. "Take it."

"What's in it?" I asked.

Her eyes widened as she growled at me, the sound contorted and deep.

Axel suddenly grabbed my arm and pulled me away from her.

She started crying loudly. I covered my mouth to silence my sob as her back arched off the ground.

"No!" I cried. "Please, don't let this happen to her."

But the Goddess didn't reply; she did nothing as we watched Natalie begin to transform, her eyes shifting from blue to red and then back. "Don't let me—die one as—one of them," she begged. "Let me die... as an Enchanted."

I pulled away from Axel.

Axel stepped forward, his claws at the ready to kill her.

I pushed him out of the way. "Don't touch her! Don't... don't touch her. I'll do it." I looked down at her, my eyes blurry with tears. "I'll do it." I held her stare for a moment, my hands shaking at my sides.

She slowly stopped crying. Her eyes stopped changing color and remained blue as her body stopped bending in all angles.

Xavier rushed into the room, his eyes darting around before landing on Natalie, and he raised his hands to sink his fingers into his hair. "Natalie?" he called in shock, his eyes instantly tearing up.

She turned her head to him, a weak smile appearing on her lips before she looked my way once more.

"Don't burn her, Ruby," he called to me.

"I won't," I replied, my voice cracking and barely audible. "I'm so sorry. I love you, Natalie."

Her eyes slowly closed, the smile still on her lips as she took her last breath.

We all stood there in silence for what felt like forever.

I couldn't cry, I couldn't move, and I couldn't look away from her.

She was gone. Natalie, my best friend—was gone.

"What did you do to her?" Presley asked, his voice heavy with emotion.

I closed my eyes. "I put her to sleep and then stopped her heart," I answered before opening my eyes and picking up the box, her blood on the bottom dripping on the ground as I headed away from the room.

When I stepped out of the room, Mathieu, along with a few other soldiers and werewolves, was being carried to the infirmary on a stretcher. I stopped them, and moving from one person to the next, I healed them all, Natalie's box still in one hand.

I felt numb, as if I was just going through the motions without any conscious thought or intention.

Everyone stayed silent, their watchful eyes filled with sadness and pity.

It became too much for me. After everyone was healed, I walked to Natalie's room, her sweet scent filling my nostrils as I stepped through the door.

Clutching her box to my chest, I sank to the floor by her bed and started screaming until my throat felt sore and could no longer make any sounds. Then I just laid on the floor and sobbed until I had no tears left.

•••• •••

AXEL

No one was talking.

We had won a major victory against the vampires by killing another General, but it didn't feel like we had won. It felt like we had lost.

Ruby hadn't left Natalie's room since yesterday when it all happened, and Xavier hadn't said a word to anyone. The entire Blackmoon Pack had been silent, their eyes reflecting the grief within them. I only recently became acquainted with Natalie, but I recognized right away that she was a good woman who cared deeply for her family and her pack. So many other lives were lost as well, both human and werewolf.

I made my way to the command room.

Xavier, Mathieu, and General Presley were there.

"If we're attacked again, we'll be wiped out," Presley remarked to me as I joined them. "We don't have enough men, and it's going to take some time before reinforcements get here. More than half of my men are..." He sighed as the muscles in his jaws clenched. "We've both lost too many people," he said sadly to Mathieu.

Xavier turned away. "And we still don't know where the Queen is."

"Right now," I finally spoke, "we need to get the manpower before even thinking about the Queen. Presley's right. If we're attacked right now, we're all dead, and the Queen wins." I sat down and crossed my legs.

No one spoke for a moment until Xavier turned back around, his hand on his chin. "One werewolf pack isn't enough."

I sat up as he said this, my eyes narrowed with interest. "What are you saying?"

"We need to ask the other packs for help," he explained.

It was a good idea, but also one that had a very small chance of working. "My pack will help. Getting the other packs to come out of hiding and do the same—let alone work alongside humans— won't be easy."

Mathieu began drumming his fingers on the table. "It might be easier than you think."

I frowned. "How so? Right now, werewolves hate humans more than ever. No offense," I gestured to Presley.

He shrugged. "None taken. I get it. What are you thinking, Mathieu? Do you have a way to get them to help us?"

"Not me," Mathieu replied as he looked from Presley, to Xavier, and then to me. "Ruby."

Xavier stepped forward, his arms crossed over his chest.

I know he was feeling protective of her right now because I felt the same way. What she did in that parking lot—controlling the weather like that—I'd never seen anything like it. On the one hand, it seemed as if there was nothing she couldn't do. However, we had both seen the lost look in her eyes the moment she had to end Natalie's life. She needed time to heal from something like that.

I could feel the emptiness within her.

"I don't think we should bother her right now. She needs some time to herself. What could she possibly do to get all the packs here anyways?" Xavier asked.

"We tell them who she is," Mathieu mumbled more to himself before nodding, as if his own idea suddenly made sense. "We need to let the other packs know who she is, who her mother was, and that she has divinity. She's the one chosen by our goddess for this; they *will* follow her. We have no reason to keep hiding who she is."

"He's right," I agreed. "And I think it would be best to keep her distracted right now."

Xavier clenched his jaws as he looked my way. He bit down on his lip, his eyes darting back and forth thoughtfully. "Okay, but why not take another step forward and ask the other supernaturals for help. Werewolves and humans can't win this war alone when there are vampires that can manipulate the weather, even with Ruby on our side. Her job is to kill the Queen, but there are still tons of vampires to get through to *get* to the Queen. We need more power on our side."

"I can do it."

We looked around and found Ruby standing behind us.

I hadn't even smelled her. "Your scent... I didn't smell you." I looked her up and down.

Stepping forward, her face looked pale, and her eyes were a little swollen. Her expression showed no emotions of sadness or anger; her eyes looked appeared dull and devoid of emotion.

I hated it.

"I masked it." She sighed. "It's as if each time I'm forced to use a large amount of my powers, something else gets unlocked. I, um, I can do it. I can try to contact the other werewolves and ask for help."

"There is one problem," Presley said. "We won't be able to spread the information fast enough. Cell phone towers are down or barely working."

"That won't be needed," Ruby replied. She opened the box in her hand and then closed it.

"Is that something that can help?" Xavier asked.

She shrugged. "Natalie told me to trust my powers and a door will be opened for me. I've been thinking about it, and maybe she meant a literal door. I, um..." She swallowed hard as she looked away. "I think she knew she was going to die." She glanced at Xavier. "The way she knew we were going to be attacked that night."

"Then the Goddess allowed her to die," Xavier replied, his eyes changing to black.

Ruby only sighed. "Yes, she did, but now we have to make sure

Natalie didn't die in vain. Wherever this door is, when I find it, maybe I'll get some straight answers about how to end this."

Xavier and I shared a look because we both already knew how this had ended the first time. What if Ruby learned about the werewolf that had died after becoming The Goddess's vessel? I would not survive watching Ruby die.

"Yeah." I stood up. "Let's just start with how to get the other packs here."

CHAPTER TWELVE
RUBY

Presley took us all to a room much like the one the Bleeder was kept in. The room was smaller than the Bleeder's had been, and didn't have a cage. While I entered, the guys stayed in the observation room.

I felt so numb inside and so tired. I hadn't been able to leave Natalie's room after I had closed her door behind me; therefore, I hadn't eaten anything in hours. I couldn't even think about food —not when she was gone, especially not when I'd ultimately been the one to take her life.

I wanted it to be me who fulfilled her request to ensure she felt as little pain as possible as she passed. I wanted to be the one to grant her final wish of dying as herself, as an Enchanted, but it killed me inside that it had to happen. I believe now that Natalie had known it would happen, and that hurt even worse. I wanted to be angry that she had kept something like that from us— something that could have been prevented had we only known— but I didn't have the strength to be angry.

I just missed her—I missed her so much.

"Ruby, did you hear me?" Presley's voice echoed in the room.

I turned to the clear glass separating me from the guys and shook my head. "No, sorry. What did you say?"

"I said we'll be right here if you need any help," he repeated.

I nodded as I pulled the chair out from behind the desk, the only furniture in the room, and sat down. Placing the box on the table gently, I stared at it for a moment as I exhaled through my mouth before opening it.

Inside laid a silver dagger, its handle encrusted in dazzling crystals. The first time I opened the box, I immediately closed it. The energy it emitted called to me, but what was scary to me was how it somehow felt familiar.

I could see myself in the shiny, double-bladed steel. The longer I looked, the more the urge to pick it up grew. As I grabbed the dagger, the blade instantly started to glow. As a peaceful feeling of security washed over me, my hold on it grew tighter.

"We're right here, okay? Just call out if you need us."

Xavier's voice over the intercom broke the trance-like state I was in. I didn't bother looking. I just nodded and placed my other hand on the handle as I closed my eyes.

"I know," I finally answered after a moment.

I placed the tip of the blade onto the table and remained in that position, my hands wrapped around the pleasantly warm crystals. After a few minutes, I cracked an eye open.

"Nothing is happening." My other eye opened, and I looked down at the dagger, its blade still glowing. "Maybe this thing is just a knife that glows."

"Remember what I told you when you were trying to locate Presley?" Axel asked. "Don't force something to happen, Ruby. Let it happen."

I rolled my shoulders as I adjusted myself on the chair. "Okay," I replied as I exhaled through my mouth. "I can do this."

I closed my eyes and relaxed my grip on the knife. I focused on the way my power was reacting to the energy coming from the knife—on the feeling of peace within my heart, the weightlessness of it. My chest had been feeling tight yet hollow ever since Natalie, and what I felt now had my eyes stinging with tears.

I wasn't ready to feel peace, not yet; not until I avenged Natalie's death and all of this was over. I opened my eyes, ready to give up on the dagger, but the room I sat in slowly faded away around me. I looked to the guys and found them standing there, their watchful eyes on me. Then they faded away like the rest of my surroundings, and I found myself seated at a table in the meadow. I recognized it as the same meadow where I saw Lovette.

I got up quickly, turning in a circle as I looked for her. "Lovette?" I called. "Mom?"

"She's not here," a voice informed me.

I spun around to find a woman standing behind me.

The large white cloak she wore covered her body entirely. I bent down somewhat to see the face hidden by the large hood over her head, but all I could make out was darkness in the space a face should be.

My hold on the knife tightened. "Who are you?"

"I have many names," she answered, her voice echoing softly around me. "And no name."

My eyes widened. "You're—you're the Goddess, aren't you?"

"It's nice to finally meet you, Ruby," she responded.

I sighed. *So this is the Goddess, the woman who fucked up my life completely.*

"That wasn't my intention," she contended.

I froze. "Don't do that. Don't read my mind."

She tilted her head to the side, her face still in darkness. "As you wish," she replied.

"Is this yours?" I waved the knife.

She nodded. "It is. It was given to Natalie as a means for her to contact me."

My jaw clenched as she said Natalie's name. She didn't deserve to talk about Natalie after what she allowed to happen to her.

"She's dead," I responded through clenched teeth. "But you must know that."

"I know. She's at peace now," she replied calmly.

I shook my head. I know I should probably show more reverence or whatever, standing in the presence of a goddess, but honestly, I was too pissed to be submissive. "You could have saved her," I pointed out, my voice cracking as I got emotional.

The front of her cloak moved away as her hands moved to her shoulder to push the garment over her shoulder.

I couldn't stop staring at her arms. Her skin looked black with bright dazzling stars, and I felt like I was staring at the night sky. She was wearing white armor that covered her breasts, knee-high silver boots, and a white shirt and shorts with silver chains on them. Her legs were covered in stars like her arms, and her stomach was bare. I frowned at an odd marking like the moon where her navel should be that appeared to be actually moving on her skin.

She was beautiful. I couldn't help wondering what her face looked like. "Are there other gods like you?" I questioned her as I looked away from her stomach to her hooded face.

"Yes," she answered. "Many. I was appointed to handle the situation on your earth."

"My earth?" I repeated, and then I remembered the witch who had said there were other worlds. "Oh, right, okay then. Why did you save me?"

"Out of all my descendants, Lovette was my favorite. She... valued all life, and she understood many things on a higher level. She asked for my help, I presented her with the terms, and she agreed."

"Okay. Why am I mated to both Xavier and Axel? What does that have to do with all of this?"

She inhaled as a meteor shower flashed across her chest.

I couldn't stop my eyes from widening in astonishment, but her chuckle caused me to look away quickly.

"I apologize. I know my skin can be quite distracting." She moved her cloak so it covered her again.

I had to admit I felt disappointed by this; her skin was just so mesmerizing.

"You were destined to be mated to Xavier at birth," she explained. "It was after Axel lost his first love that I mated you to him. His family played a part in the previous war, and he has his role to play in this one. The Bluewater and Blackmoon packs needed to come together once more, and both humans and werewolves needed to see that a union between both species is possible and allowed."

"So our bond is meant to bring the packs back together, and also, what... um, start a new era between humans and supernaturals?"

"Precisely. As you've all now realized, Amythia can't be killed without the species of Earth uniting," she replied.

I held my hand up for her to stop. "Wait, hold on just a minute, the vampire Queen's name is Amythia? Why does it take someone like me to kill her, anyway? Is she that powerful?" I questioned.

"She's a demigod."

I blinked and said nothing while I tried to process this new information. After a moment I nodded. "Yeah okay, that makes sense. So why can't one of you just kill her, then?"

"Gods can walk among you, but not for long periods. We can enter your minds, but to use a vessel, it has to be strong enough to contain our divinity. Otherwise it dies rather quickly. Amythia's lineage began from a goddess and the father of demons in a rather... gruesome and barbaric manner we don't need to discuss."

I made a face. "That's fine."

"Therefore, her kind is particularly hard to kill. The first of her kind was banned from both her father's realm and ours," she added.

I snorted. "So, we're stuck with her. Wonderful, that's great," I said sarcastically as I looked down at the knife in my hand. "How do I kill her, and how do I contact all the other werewolves?"

"You can mind link all of them. You have my power, Ruby, an abundance of it, so you're capable of many great things if you trust yourself. Nevertheless, when the time comes to take Amythia's life, you will accept me. You'll become my vessel, and then I will kill her."

I took a breath, the sound of this not sitting well with me. "So, I'll have to do the same thing that has probably killed a ton of other vessels? That's great; so will I survive, then? Since I'm different?"

"No," she replied bluntly. "You were born of a powerful Enchanted and a human and were given divinity at birth. You're strong, Ruby, the strongest supernatural I've seen in a long time, and I am proud of you for all you have done and survived so far. Yet, no matter how strong you are, you cannot survive having all my divinity. There are some positives, though. You will reunite with your mother and Natalie when this is all over."

My brows knitted tightly. I had nothing to say, so I walked away.

"You were saved for this purpose," she went on. "To be my earthly vessel."

"I wasn't given a choice," I muttered under my breath.

"When the time comes, you will have to pierce your heart with that dagger. This is the only way to end Amythia, Ruby."

I shook my head, no longer finding the warmth from the dagger comforting. "I won't do it," I said softly before turning around. "I won't do it. I can't give you my body. Don't you get it? My life has never been mine, never! Now, I'm expected to give my body and my life away too?"

"Your body will die, but your spirit will live on with the gods," she added.

I laughed humorlessly as I looked around the meadow. My face fell as the flowers around us started to die.

"Or would you prefer I take back my divinity and you die now?" she asked. "Mind you, if you choose death now, your soul will be erased. You will not pass on, you will simply cease to exist."

The sky above us grew dark.

I clenched my fists. If she was trying to scare me, it was working, but I refused to be used any longer. She gave me this power, and I would use it to kill Amythia. I would do it my way with the help of the werewolves and every other supernatural.

I can't give my body up, I just can't do it!

"Choose!" The Goddess yelled, her voice like a clap of thunder rumbling from the sky. "Make a choice, child, and I will find someone else to save your world!"

My lips parted as I watched the Goddess approach me. As much as I wanted to run for my life, where would I run to? Also, why was she bothering to give me a choice and not simply taking her power back?

"Take it, then!" I blurted out.

She stopped in front of me.

"Take your divinity back, and let me die here. I'll cease to exist, and you'll still have the vampires to deal with," I yelled as thunder echoed loudly above us. I nodded as I exhaled heavily. "You can't do it. You can't take back what you've given me. I have to give it back willingly. Right? You can't possess my body without me permitting you."

"You're either incredibly brave or incredibly stupid, girl," the Goddess grumbled, her voice now deep and dark.

Goosebumps dotted my flesh just from her voice. "I pick brave," I said softly.

She turned on her heel, her cloak billowing around her, and she vanished.

The ground beneath me started to crack. As I ran towards the table and chair still sitting in the meadow, the ground opened up, and I fell in.

Have you ever had a dream where you're suddenly falling and you startle awake? That's how it felt as I fell into darkness.

My back hit cold, hard ground. I opened my eyes to see I was back at the army base.

The door flew open and the guys rushed in.

"Ruby? Ruby? Are you okay?" Xavier yelled in my face, his eyes wide and frantic as he looked me over.

"Can you hear us, Red? What happened?" Axel questioned from my other side.

I slowly pushed myself up into a sitting position, both of them helping me. My mouth felt dry, and my tongue felt like sandpaper. I cleared my throat as I rubbed at my aching head. "I saw the Goddess."

They all grew silent.

I looked up to see Presley looking down at me with eager blue eyes. "To kill the Queen, I'll have to become her vessel—"

"No!" Xavier announced before I even finished speaking. "You can't do it."

"We'll find another way," Axel added, but he suddenly stood. He staggered backward as he placed his hand over his chest, his hazel eyes turning black.

I looked him up and down with concern. "Axel? What is it?"

"Something's wrong," He looked towards the door. "Something's wrong with my father, I can feel it. I have to go." He headed out.

I hurried to my feet.

"Wait," Presley called out to him. "I'll have a helicopter take you, it'll be faster."

"Okay," Axel replied as he walked back over to me, pulled me into his arms, and kissed me hard. He released me after a moment. "I have to check on my pack, but I'll be back. Just please don't do anything foolish until then, okay?"

I stared into his hazel orbs. "I make no promises." I breathed the words out.

He kissed my forehead then nodded to Xavier, who did the same in response, and left with Presley.

Xavier and I stood in silence for a moment.

I turned to him, my lips parting to say something.

He shook his head. "No," he said decisively.

I frowned. "You have no idea what I was going to say," I countered.

Xavier bent forward and kissed my cheek. "We can't go with him. He can handle his pack on his own. Right now, I want to know everything that happened with the Goddess, and don't leave anything out."

CHAPTER THIRTEEN
RUBY

Even though it was midday, my skin tingled with goosebumps as a chill ran through me. I got to my knees slowly. My legs felt weak as I stared at Natalie's grave.

A quick ceremony was held yesterday. I surprisingly managed to make it through the service without having a mental breakdown. What I think allowed that to happen was my rage. The vampires had taken so much from everyone, both human and nonhuman. People had lost their family and friends to those monsters, and it had to come to an end.

I closed my eyes for a moment as the wind picked up around me, and I couldn't help wondering if it was Natalie's spirit.

"I miss you," I whispered as I listened to the wind in the oak tree above her grave. "I did what you told me. I opened a door, and I spoke to her—the Goddess. I can't do what she wants, Nat. I just can't do it." I opened my eyes. "I don't want to die," I finally admitted to even myself. "I want to see this all through and be alive to see the world that comes next. I want to be a part of this world, to make it better. She gave me the power to help, but we're the ones down here fighting, winning and losing ourselves and the ones we love, only for her to jump in at the end to claim Amythia's life? Hell no. I want to take Amythia down, and I want to be alive to celebrate when this is all over. Haven't I earned that after everything I've survived and sacrificed? If I only get control over one thing in life, it should be my own body!"

I sighed as some of my anger dissipated. I sat there for a moment as I reflected on the conversation I had with the Goddess. For now, I had to keep fighting the fight. To win, or even begin to have enough strength on our side to stand a chance, I had to mind link with the other wolves.

"I wish you were here right now. I really could've used your help with this." I sat down on the ground and bent my legs lotus-style.

My shoulders rose as I inhaled deeply and then dropped as I exhaled. Closing my eyes, I tried to remember how I felt the first time Natalie had mind linked with me.

I stepped into that pool of power within me, sinking slowly at the deep end until I felt full. My body felt electrified, and I focused on that feeling as I thought of Xavier as well. I thought of my intentions, what I needed my power to do. I inhaled sharply as I was thrust into his mind. Images began to flash in my mind, even some of myself but seen through his eyes, and I grimaced as I felt a strain on my mind.

I clenched and unclenched my fists as I tried to gain control of myself, to not push myself too far into his mind. I didn't want to spy on his thoughts and feelings. I just wanted to communicate with him.

I soon noticed that his thoughts were all cocooned in some kind of pale blue light.

"His aura," I whispered to myself as I opened my eyes. Similar blue lights like Xavier's started appearing within my mind, and with it, I could feel each wolf.

I smiled widely as I located more and more wolves. My hands

still clenched and unclenched to help keep me balanced. I tried not to get carried away by the exhilarating feeling.

"Natalie, I did..." I started to say, but when my eyes landed on her grave, my face fell. Right, she wasn't really here with me.

The feeling of elation I experienced vanished as I tried to not lose focus. I exhaled as I released my clenched fists and continued mind linking with each werewolf, their bright lights filling my mind. It was as if I stood in a white room, surrounded by floating blue lights, each representing a person.

"Hello," I greeted them. "My name is Ruby, and maybe some of you have heard of me. For those who haven't, let me introduce myself. I'm Ruby Saunders, the daughter of the late and beloved Grand Elder, Lovette."

Soft whispers came from each light.

I continued speaking, "I will make this short because time is of the essence. I'm half-human, half-Enchanted, and my mother hid me from the world so that one day, I could help to save it. Yes, I'm a half-breed, but one blessed by the Goddess herself, blessed with her divinity to help with the destruction of the vampire threat."

The whispers grew louder.

I felt rushed but I kept speaking, "I know this is confusing and you're all scared, but the vampires are growing stronger while we cower and hide. Soon, we won't stand a chance against them. Why should we wait until that happens before we band together and take back our world? The humans were wrong for hunting us. They have now seen the error of their ways. I will never overlook or forget the bloodshed they lent a hand in. I can feel your pain, all of you, and I'm sorry, I'm so very sorry about what you've all had to endure. Long ago, werewolves and humans came together to battle these creatures, and they won. We can do that again, but only if we come together. Humans and werewolves can unite, and I'm proof of that. Lovette proved that the moment she fell in love with a human, the moment she gave birth to me." I exhaled heavily. "I wasn't looked down on by the Goddess for not being a pure-blood. Instead, she blessed me. Despite the power I possess from the divinity she gave me, I can't do this alone. None of us can do this alone. I'm tired of watching the ones I love die! Aren't you? If we do nothing, more lives will be lost, and our pain will only grow worse! We have to stand together, and not just survive this, but end it. You must recognize that this *is* an invasion of vampires bent on the dominion over and obliteration of all other species, and if we do nothing, we will all die!" I turned in a circle, blue auras all around me to the towering ceiling in the room glowing brighter than before. "Werewolves have always been protectors because of their strength and power," I said more softly. "I'm asking you all to be those guardians again. You all now know my location and that I'm the mate to both Xavier of the Blackmoon Pack and Axel of the Bluewater Pack. Join us, and let us put an end to this. Let's remind these bloodsuckers of our true power, and that they are nothing compared to us!"

Cheers were coming from each light, the room coming alive with their howls and roars.

"Their power is nothing compared to ours! This is our world, and we're ready to take it back!" I took a sharp intake of breath as my eyes opened, and I was once more sitting at Natalie's grave. My breathing was labored as I wiped away a tear from my cheek. I hadn't even realized I was crying, but I had been able to feel the emotions of all those werewolves. Their pain and sorrow flowed through me as if their emotions were my own.

I hugged myself as I leaned forward, fresh tears streaming down my cheeks. Was this what the Goddess had to endure, so many emotions from so many wolves?

A blue light flashed within my mind, and I instantly knew it was Xavier. I looked behind me to find him standing there with the pack, their eyes all on me. I got up quickly while wiping at my tears, but there was no point in trying to hide it.

"We all heard you," a woman informed me, her eyes red with unshed tears.

"We're proud to have you as a part of our pack, Ruby," a man added as he stepped forward.

"Luna," another man said, followed by another, and soon, they were all calling me their Luna as I was pulled into one hug after another.

I didn't know what to do or say.

Xavier stood off to the side, a smile on his lips.

I awkwardly hugged everyone. Never had I felt so much love aimed at me. I guessed this was what it must feel like to have a family.

They all surrounded me, some thanking me for healing them from when the vampires had attacked.

After a while, it was just Xavier and me.

We stood in silence as we both stared at Natalie's grave.

"Do you think she's watching us?" He broke the quiet.

I smiled. "I know she is, and I know she's at peace. The Goddess said Natalie and my mom are both with her."

He hummed his response as he took my hand.

We walked back to the base slowly.

I pressed myself to his side.

Throwing his hand over my shoulder, he pulled me closer and kissed the top of my head. "How are you feeling after doing that? You really pulled it off."

I grinned at the pride in his voice. "I feel okay, good actually. I could feel them; I could feel all of you." I stopped walking.

So did he.

I turned to look up at him. "They were all so petrified."

"You just changed that," he told me as he moved my hair behind my ear. "You reminded them that they aren't weaklings and gave them hope. I'm proud of you."

I hugged him, and he crushed me to his hard chest as he kissed the top of my head. I melted in his arms as I listened to his steady heartbeat. "What if I have to do what—"

"No," he shot back before I had even finished speaking.

I looked up at him, resting my chin on his chest.

"No," he repeated.

"But what if I have to do what she wants? What if I can't kill the Queen on my own, and I have to become the Goddess's vessel?" As much as the thought of giving up my body made me feel nauseous, I needed to consider the chance that I might have to do it.

I was just welcomed by the Blackmoon pack as their Luna. They were all my responsibility now, and if other packs turned up, they would also be here because of me. They would have all come out of hiding because I asked them to, so what would happen if I couldn't kill the Queen? We'd lose this war, and the lives lost would be my fault.

I couldn't live with that.

"I just asked thousands of werewolves to put their faith in me, to fight with me. There is no room for failure, Xavier. We failed in our raid of that coven, thinking the Queen was there, and we lost so many because of it, including Natalie. I can't let them down. If I have to die to keep my word, I will."

He held my shoulders firmly, his head shaking wildly. "Never say that, Ruby, never! You aren't going to die, and you won't have to sacrifice yourself. Do you understand me? I won't let that happen, ever. Demigod or not, we can and will kill her together. Okay?"

I couldn't look away from the emotions within his eyes, his fear of losing me so raw I could almost feel it within me.

"Okay? Promise me you won't use that dagger," he pleaded.

"Okay," I agreed as I looked down.

Desperate, he grabbed my chin.

"Okay, I promise, I won't use it."

"I cannot lose you, Ruby. I can't—not you, too," he rambled out a little. "I won't." He kissed me, long, hard, and passionately, his love and emotions transferring to me in waves.

I wasn't sure what came over me, but I pulled away and the

words left my lips before I could stop them. "I love you." My eyes widened as I heard what I had said, and I tried to step out of his arms.

Xavier tightened his hold on me, his eyes turning black. He kissed me again, his elongated fangs grazing my lips somewhat.

I didn't care. I wanted to feel him, taste him, and I had meant what I had just said. Natalie had told me to be honest about my feelings, tell the people I love that I loved them. I couldn't stand that she had died thinking I was angry at her.

From the start, Xavier had been looking out for me; he'd been saving my life from the moment we met. The Goddess had said I was mated to him at birth, so he'd always been the one for me. I knew I loved him, body and soul.

"I love you, too," he whispered against my lips as he pulled away. "My Luna."

I grinned. "I like the sound of that."

———————•● ◐•———————

XAVIER

Two wolves walked by me and nodded their greeting, but their brows were furrowed in curiosity. No doubt, they were wondering why I was grinning like a damn idiot.

From the moment those three words had left Ruby's lips yesterday, I hadn't been able to stop smiling. However, that wasn't the only thing I had to be happy about. Everyone was in high spirits, the air thick with the smell of hope. A few hours after Ruby had mind linked with all the wolves, some of them had found us. By dusk more arrived, and now, at midday the following day, another pack of forty-five wolves arrived.

Presley had also confirmed that military reinforcements were being sent and would arrive within a day. Being unable to travel through the night was a bother, but it was better to be late than dead.

The way I saw it, the people joining us now weren't late. On the contrary, they were right on time. Ruby had been trying her best to be sociable with everyone, but she didn't exactly enjoy being treated as if she were royalty. Unfortunately, extra attention was to be expected when you were the daughter of Grand Elder Lovette and blessed by our goddess. I couldn't be prouder to be her mate, but she was clearly uncomfortable being in the spotlight.

Despite the mask of sociability she wore, I could tell that she was anxious about Axel. He hadn't returned, and we had no way of contacting him. She tried mind linking with him last night, but after doing it on such a large scale, she wasn't able to connect with him.

"Xavier, more werewolves have arrived. They traveled through the night to get here," a soldier said as he approached me, a pile of towels in hand.

"What's with the towels? Are they hurt? They shouldn't have traveled through the night," I wondered.

He shook his head. "No, they are fine. Just raining outside," he answered with a smile. "There are kids in the group, so they need these."

"Oh, okay." I nodded and he carried on. "Hey," I called after him. "Thanks for the help."

"Don't mention it!" he replied before leaving.

The tension between my pack and the humans when we first arrived was now all but gone. For the wolves that had arrived recently, it would take some time for them to be as comfortable, but I trusted that we'd get there.

I kept walking slowly as I headed to Ruby's room, my hands buried in my pockets. No way in hell would I allow her to use the dagger to accept the Goddess. She promised to not do it, but I needed to keep an eye on her.

I stopped walking, my brows pulling together, as I came upon an odd scent. It was there one second and then gone another. I started walking fast, as a sense of dread filled my chest. Once I got to Ruby's room, I opened the door without knocking.

My heart skipped a beat at the sight of her floating above her bed, her long red hair dancing around her body. A vampire's scent immediately filled my nostrils as I turned to the window, and sure enough, the General we saw before, the one who had walked away from us, was suspended in the air outside her window.

I rushed forward as he moved his hand, calling Ruby forward, and she started drifting to the window. I dove at her to knock her out of the air, but her body floated higher and I missed. I collided into the wall, cracks appearing from the impact.

I hurried to my feet as her body slipped through the window. Without thinking, without hesitating, I dove through the window, my hand outstretched to her. Alas, my claws merely scratched her ankle as I fell.

I started shifting midair, howling to issue a warning to the others. By the time I landed on the ground, I had completely shifted. Though I registered the pain of the impact, I rose quickly even as I felt some cracked bones begin to heal. I started running through the forest, my head up as I tried to follow them. I howled to her, praying she would hear me and wake up from whatever sleep the vampire had put her in.

After two minutes of following them, they vanished from my sight. I swiped my claws at a tree trunk in rage, shredding it as three other transformed wolves joined me. I started shifting back, and the pain of my bones re-breaking was nothing compared to the pain in my chest.

I was reminded of the agony I had to endure when Axel had taken her, a pain I never wanted to feel again. Turning to face my father's wolf, I closed my eyes for a moment as my rage started to get out of control, my wolf in a panic. "We have to find her," I growled as I opened my eyes.

My father released a growl before turning to run back to the base. The others followed him.

I peered up at the sky, my clenched fists shaking at my sides before I took off in a run.

• • •

XAVIER

My fist came down hard on the table, breaking it in half. The room went silent, and I turned away. Combing my hand through my hair, I tried to get my wolf under control. When I turned back around to face the others, my eyes were back to their normal steel gray.

"We can find her," Presley stated confidently.

I pinned him with a glare. I wasn't angry at him (and he knew it), but right now, I wanted to rip the world and everyone in it apart until I found her.

"How?" Randoll, our pack's Beta, asked as he combed his curly red hair out of his face. His scarlet locks just flopped right back down, no matter what he did to try to control them.

"I had her ingest a tracker when she arrived," Presley replied.

"You did *what*?" I saw red and rushed forward, but my father stepped in front of Presley. A deep resounding growl emitted from him as his dominance filled the room.

Randoll and the three other wolves within the room lowered their heads submissively.

I fought against it for a moment before doing the same. The difference between the other wolves and me was that I did it out of respect, as I could easily defy him now. My strength had grown immensely over these last few months. "Why?" I asked through clenched teeth.

"For a scenario exactly like this one. I knew we weren't the only people who were interested in her, and her safety was mission-critical. She's also not the only person with a tracking device, Xavier. I wouldn't do that to her. I have one, as do many of our higher-ranking officers."

"Does she know?" I asked as I held my head up.

My dad stepped to the side, revealing Presley once more.

"No, I thought it would be best to not say anything in case she got the wrong idea and refused, but our eyes have to be on an asset like Ruby at all times," he responded. The facial tic I experienced at hearing him call her 'an asset' had him clearing his throat. "She's special to us all. I understand to you and Axel more so, but her safety means everything to me as well. We can stand here and argue about this, or you can let me help with finding her."

"Your men that went with Axel, have they reported anything back yet?"

He shook his head. "No, we lost contact with them." He then stepped over a leg of the broken table on the ground.

We all walked to the command room quickly, and I tried to contain my anxiety as I allowed Presley and his people to do their work. However, I couldn't stop myself from stepping forward the moment a red dot appeared on one of the screens with a map and began beeping. "Is that her?" I narrowed my eyes at the screen.

"Yes," Presley replied. "It looks like they are going north."

"We have to go get her, now." The sooner we got moving to go get her, the sooner I could get her back where I could protect her.

How could I have let this happen?

My dad placed his hand on my shoulder. "We can't go after her half-cocked, Xavier, and you know that. No doubt she's being taken to Amythia, and if that's the case, we need to be prepared. We need to gather everyone before we can go there. We have no idea what we'll be walking into."

I could understand the reasoning behind his words and that they rang with truth, but I needed to get her back. The more time we wasted, the more her chances of being killed by the Queen increased. "I hear you, I do, but we can't wait any longer. The

Queen is going to kill her, Dad. We promised… I promised Ruby that I'd be there with her—I'd fight this war with her; all of us. If she's forced to fight the Queen alone, the Queen will kill her, or the Goddess will."

"I'm not giving my men the order to leave, Xavier," Presley replied. "I'm sorry, but rushing in will get her and us killed."

I stared at him, my face no doubt turning red. My wolf was clawing at my insides, panicked that even right now she might be suffering.

If Axel were here, he would share my feelings that we needed to act now. I shook my head. "It's like you all don't understand that she's going to die."

"Xavier, we understand that. I know how you feel, son, I do, but listen to—"

"The only way Ruby can kill the Queen is by killing herself!" I yelled.

The command room grew silent.

My dad frowned. "What are you talking about?"

Axel and I never told anyone about what Malcolm had found in the book, that Ruby would have to become the Goddess's vessel. Ruby didn't know I already knew that detail before she spoke to the Goddess.

There was no more room for secrets, however.

"When Ruby becomes the Goddess's vessel, it'll kill her. She won't survive it," I answered. "If she's forced to fight the Queen alone, she'll have no choice but to do it, and we'll lose her." I ran my hand down my face. "Either the Goddess kills her or Amythia does, but the only chance we have of her surviving this is if we're there with her, if we fight with her!"

"But she's been living with the Goddess's divinity. She's capable of killing vampires. We've all seen it," Presley argued.

I shook my head. "Amythia isn't just a vampire. She's a demigod, and the power Ruby has now will be nothing compared to how powerful she'll be once the Goddess enters her body.

That's the kind of power that will be necessary to defeat Amythia without our help." I nodded to Randoll as I walked to the door.

He and the other wolves in the room followed me.

I wasn't going to lose her, not to the Goddess or this damn war. "The price for the Goddess' power is Ruby's life, and she shouldn't have to pay that price to save us all. I'm leaving, Presley. You and your men can stay, but Ruby is one of us. She's our Luna. More than that, she's my mate. I'm going to go get her, and there's not a thing anyone can do to stop me."

CHAPTER FOURTEEN
RUBY

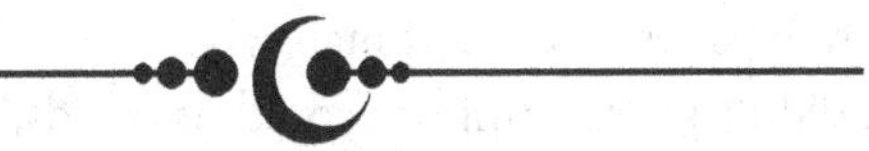

I stretched and rolled to my side before I realized my bed felt different. My eyes cracked open, and I instantly sat up, becoming a little dizzy from the sudden movement.

I couldn't look away from the woman and man staring at me, my eyes looking from one to the other.

The man wore a vampire General's uniform and I had a strong feeling he was the one who'd been trying to see into my mind. His hair was a dusty blonde skimmed his ears and his red eyes narrowed the more I stared at him. He looked to be over six feet.

My eyes drifted to the woman. Surprisingly, she was even taller than he was. I was stunned by her beauty.

Her black hair was bone straight and fell below her bottom. Her skin looked milky white, almost as white as the dress she wore, but it was her red eyes that did it for me. They were completely red —pupils, irises, and sclera. A chill went down my spine as she smiled at me and flashed her pointy fangs.

"It's so lovely to finally meet you, Ruby," she greeted me, her voice so sweet and soft.

Despite her pleasant voice and appearance, instinctively I knew that there was nothing sweet or soft about this woman.

What I saw before me was the perfect predator—stunning, with an allure that would draw anyone to her. That is, until they found themselves hopelessly tangled in her web of lies and deceit.

"I'm Queen Amythia." She then waved her hand towards the General at her side. "This is General Carden, my firstborn son. I think you've already met, haven't you?" she asked him, and he nodded. "Good. Now that we've all been introduced, let's get down to business, as you humans say."

"I didn't know vampires could have kids," I retorted, deciding to ignore what she had said about getting down to business. It was taking all my strength to keep my heartbeat steady. I didn't want her to have the satisfaction of knowing I was afraid of her.

Her red-painted lips stretched with a wide smile. "There is a lot that's not known about vampires."

"Aren't you all dead? So how can you give birth?" I questioned.

She laughed. The sound was soft and beautiful, sensual even, as she walked to a chair at the other end of the room.

My eyes slid to Carden for a moment and caught his eyes roaming my body. I pinned him with a glare, and the corner of his mouth twitched with a smirk.

"I didn't give birth to him the way humans do." She sat down and crossed her legs at the ankle. "I turned him personally. He's one of three sons that I've turned over the years." Her face suddenly fell. "One of which you killed."

"He tried to kill me," I told her.

She glanced at Carden before looking down at her feet poking out from beneath her dress. "I see. He was given orders not to," she whispered more to herself.

Is this really the vampire Queen? I was expecting a ghastly creature, not this—not someone that appeared to be so angelic. It was her eyes that gave away her true demonic nature.

"I know what you're thinking, Ruby. My eyes bother even

some of my own." She turned to face me again. "We're not monsters or savages, you know."

I snorted.

She arched a perfect brow at me. "How things have happened is unfortunate, but we're only trying to survive. We just want a home like you and every other creature on this earth."

"You're doing that by killing every other creature. I can think of a few other ways you could have done this," I said bluntly as I shrugged.

She shook her head. "Humans never would have accepted us, and we have no intention of living like the supernaturals of this time." She took a deep breath.

I found myself wondering if she was actually breathing. I looked at Carden, and sure enough, his chest wasn't moving.

"We tried that once before, and it didn't end well, as I'm sure you now know." She leaned forward, her eyes narrowing at me. "Your scent is quite distracting."

"Let me go, and it won't be a bother to you anymore," I told her.

She chuckled. "I don't mind it that much." She glanced at Carden. "Leave us," she commanded.

He turned away after taking another long look at me.

She waited until he closed the door behind him before turning to face me. "Now, we girls can chat."

I said nothing as I stared back at her.

How am I going to get out of this one?

It had taken so much out of me to kill that other General, I ended up losing control. Here I would have to go through Carden and other skilled vampires who might be outside—not to mention Amythia herself. I knew I didn't have the power to handle all of them on my own—not without the Goddess. And I wasn't exactly eager to bring her into this if I could help it.

Carden's scent woke me from my sleep back at the base, but the moment I opened my eyes and saw him, he plunged into my mind, forcing me back to sleep. I hadn't stood a chance. How would Xavier and the others ever find me? This wasn't how I saw this going. This wasn't how this was supposed to happen. *I'm not prepared!*

"Ruby?" Amythia called. "Are you feeling okay? You look a little pale."

"Enough of this nice girl act, Amythia. Stop acting like you actually care, *Your Majesty*. What is it that you want from me?"

She reclined in her chair and ran her hand down her dress. Her nails were at least six inches long and all pointy.

I didn't want to think about all the lives those things must have taken over the years.

"Vampires and your kind didn't always hate each other, you know. There was a time when supernatural creatures and humans co-existed peacefully." She looked nostalgic as she spoke. "Those were better times."

"I know, but I also saw the war that happened," I replied.

She frowned. "You had a vision of the past?" she asked.

I nodded.

"Well, there are rules among the supernatural community, Ruby, rules that can't be broken. They were broken back then, and the world broke too. But enough about all that. What I would like right now is to see your power."

"I'd rather not do that, if you don't mind," I replied politely but firmly. I didn't like the way she was looking me up and down. I felt like an animal at a circus being told to do a trick.

Her face fell, a crease appearing between her brows as she stood up.

I quickly did the same.

"Do as I ask," she said with an edge in her voice.

I clenched my teeth as I stood my ground. I called on my power, allowing it to rest at the tips of my fingers.

I opened my mouth to speak when she suddenly blurred from

my vision. When she reappeared much closer, I jumped back in fear, and I held my hands up to defend myself.

Her mouth dislocated like that of a snake getting ready to eat a large animal, and my stomach clenched.

Amythia was no longer the beautiful queen. Now the real creature stood in front of me. Her eyes grew larger and more cat-like as black veins appeared from her neck up to her mouth. Her slick, bone-straight hair blew behind her like a black curtain, which only made her pale skin appear even whiter. She calmed down as quickly as she had become angry, and her mouth slowly went back to its normal state, the bones in her jaw snapping back into place.

"Beautiful eyes," she murmured.

I looked her up and down, my hands still up defensively. The room started to grow hot as I released my power.

She wagged a long finger at me. "There is no need for that. I merely wanted to see if you truly have the Goddess's divinity." She reached a hand out as if to touch my face and then stopped. "So much power you wield; I haven't felt divinity in a millennium. You have no idea how special you are, child." Her hand fell to her side, and the black veins on her face vanished as well. "You don't understand how much stronger you'll be if you join us."

I frowned as my hands dropped somewhat. "That's what you want... for me to become a vampire?"

She shook her head. "No, you'd be more than just a vampire. One thing that isn't widely known about vampirism is that it doesn't affect those with divinity the same way as it does other supernatural creatures. Ruby, you would retain your current abilities while gaining those that come with vampirism. You'll be the strongest creature on the earth... next to me, of course. You'd be able to topple the gods themselves."

"I don't want to become the most powerful creature on this earth!" I yelled, my obsidian eyes reflecting in her scarlet ones. "What I want is for this bloodshed to be over!"

"It never will be unless you become one of us! My Seers didn't see you before our invasion, your Goddess made sure of that, but you've changed things for the better. Join us, and all of this comes to an end. The lives of everyone you care about are in your hands, Ruby. You only have one option: join me, or die. If you choose death, I get to watch as this hellhole finally burns."

"I'd rather die than become like you!" I ran at her, the temperature inside the room instantly becoming warmer.

I didn't make it anywhere close to her before she hunched forward and a wing appeared from her back. The skin-like wing, like that of a bat, slapped me, and my entire body went flying. The sound of my shoulder blade breaking echoed in my ear as I slammed into the wall over the bed.

The side of my face hit the concrete wall so hard it cracked as I fell onto the bed, out cold.

•◦ ◦•

RUBY

I was all too familiar with the hard ground of a dungeon and the chill that comes with it. I didn't even have to open my eyes to know. It brought back memories from a confusing time at the beginning of my whole journey, but it also made me wonder if Axel was okay.

How crazy is that?

I opened my eyes and sat up slowly, happy to see that there were no chains on me. With no windows in sight and only torches outside my cell to provide light, I realized I was alone.

I sighed.

Well, that didn't go well.

As I got up, I checked my shoulder. Thankfully, it had already healed. I touched the side of my head to feel a part of my hair that felt matted. I'm sure being thrown across the room by that bitch had caused a pretty nasty wound, which fortunately appeared to have mended while I was out. I felt particularly grateful for my supernatural healing abilities right now. That head injury would've been tough to survive otherwise.

What made Amythia think I would ever become a vampire? Did she really think I'd believe her bullshit about everything coming to an end if I agreed? Who knows what would really happen to me if I turned.

"Help!" I yelled as I held onto the rusty old iron bars. "Help! Can anyone hear me?"

I knew I was doing the dumb thing everyone did in the movies, but what else was I supposed to do? I knew I had to be miles away from any human or supernatural capable of helping me.

My hands fell away from the bars as I frowned. *Why am I sitting in this cage? I'm Ruby Saunders, daughter of Lovette and vessel to a freaking goddess! I need to remember who and what I am. Why am I yelling for help?* I acted without thinking earlier and without knowing my opponent. I just couldn't believe after everything this woman had caused, all the lives lost because of her and her vampires, she'd think I'd want to join her.

I closed my eyes and listened to my breathing for a moment. I then focused on the soft crackling fire of the torches and began calling the heat from them into my palm. I reached out to touch the iron, intending to melt it and hopefully walk right through. I opened my eyes and immediately froze as red eyes stared right back at me.

A man stood outside the bars, his head tilted to the side as he watched me.

The torches had dimmed somewhat, but I could still make out his burning red eyes and blonde hair. I bared my teeth at him and reached out to grab the bars when he spoke.

"I wouldn't do that if I were you. You'd alert all of them that you're trying to escape."

"I am trying to escape, and you can go tell your Queen that. Just try to stop me, and I swear I'll fucking turn you to ash!"

He tilted his head to the other side like a curious puppy.

I frowned.

"My Queen is in purgatory," he replied.

My frown deepened. I realized he didn't smell like a vampire. "Who are you?" I kept my powers at the ready but folded my hands into fists. Unfortunately, I didn't seem to possess the same heightened senses as the rest of the werewolves. So far, I'd only been able to smell vampires and not the distinct scents of other supernaturals. Being an Enchanted, that ability could pop up sooner or later. "You're not a vampire."

"Who I am doesn't matter. I was sent by your father," he responded cryptically.

I stepped back as his body burst into a cloud of smoke. I watched as he slipped through the bars without touching them and then materialized inside the cell with me. "My presence will only go undetected for a few minutes, so we need to get moving." He held his hand out to me. "Take my hand, and don't burn me."

I hesitated as I looked from his hand to his eyes.

He made a face. "Now, Ruby. We need to go *now*." He reached out and grabbed my wrist, and before I could speak, we both turned into smoke. We floated through the bars and materialized on the other side.

"We need to hurry." He started walking quickly ahead of me. "Whenever I say take my hand, do it."

"Okay," I drawled as I walked closely behind him.

Thank you, Malcolm! How did he find me so quickly?

"My hand," the demon commanded.

I quickly grabbed his hand when I realized we were at the door to exit the dungeon. We once more turned to smoke and passed through as I eyed the two dead vampire guards by the door. "How did you find me? How did Malcolm find me?" I inquired as we ran through a dark hall. No doubt we'd be heard soon, so the sooner we got out of this place, the better.

"Do you two need directions?" Carden appeared in front of us.

We skidded to a halt.

He looked the demon up and down before looking away dismissively. His eyes then fell on me. "Did you really think you could get away that easily?" He looked me up and down as well, but the lust within his eyes was unmistakable as he inhaled deeply. "The Queen promised me your hand once you've become one of us, and you *will* become one of us. Then I will enjoy making you mine *in every way*."

I clenched my jaws tightly and tried not to think about how nauseous his comment made me.

"I might be wrong, but I think she's already taken, two times over. You're a little too late!" The demon interjected as he laughed.

Carden hissed at him as he rushed forward.

Instead of attacking him, The demon turned around and grabbed my arm. As he threw me towards the wall, I turned into smoke, and Carden slammed into him. My scream lodged itself in my throat as I came out on the other side of the wall. The freezing-cold air felt like a thousand needles poking every part of my body.

My power flared inside me as I flipped over, causing heat to flow throughout my body so I could no longer feel the cold. I realized I was falling down along a snow-covered mountain. The sounds of a battle met my ears, and I could make out transformed werewolves and vampires fighting below. The bright flash of guns being fired lit up the ground, and I knew they had to be from Presley's men.

It was daytime, but the sky was so heavily clouded, barely any sunlight was breaking through.

My quick descent slowed as I used my powers to levitate. Directly below me, three Bleeders looked up, their fangs dripping with blood. The heat I had absorbed from those torches blasted from my hands as I landed on the ground, killing them.

A wolf's thundering howl echoed, and more wolves began to

howl in response. I could feel it within me, their calls to the others of my arrival. I watched as a large brown wolf came running towards me. He rose on his hind legs and trampled a Bleeder on his way to me.

He was suddenly thrown to the side as a Skin attacked him, and I winced as the Skin bit him on the shoulder. I'd never felt Xavier's pain before, or Axel's, for that matter. A gunshot echoed so close to my body, I ducked instinctually. I felt so disoriented with everything happening around me.

Presley came running towards me, a gun in each hand. "Stay alert, Ruby. Oh, and welcome back!" He turned his back to me and raised his guns, killing two Bleeders, before looking at me over his shoulder. "I gave you a tracker! That's how we found you!" He pointed to our right.

I stared open-mouthed at an opening in the mountain, where countless Bleeders and Skins were pouring out onto the field. I looked around us at the humans and werewolves being slaughtered, and a feeling of dread rested on my chest, the scent of blood and death filling my nostrils. "We're losing!" I yelled.

I turned to our left as a Bleeder came charging at us.

Presley fired three shots into its chest.

I used my powers to send the creature flying towards the sharp rocks on the mountainside.

Xavier ran up to us, completely and unabashedly naked, with blood and cuts covering his entire body.

"Are you okay? Where is Axel?" I asked.

"I'm fine," he answered, his chest rising and falling rapidly. His eyes darted around quickly as he remained on guard. "He's not here. We lost contact with him after he left." He cupped my cheek. "If he returns to the base, he'll know to come here."

I didn't care that he'd smeared blood on me. "I felt your pain," I told him as I pointed to the bite on his shoulder. Gunshots echoed in our ears as another soldier and wolf joined us, creating somewhat of a circle around us. "If he was hurt, I think I'd know. The Queen is inside the mountain, Xavier. I saw her."

"Good. This is where this ends." His eyes were on something behind me before he quickly moved me to the side.

A chill went through my body that had nothing to do with the snow around us as I stared at the opening in the mountain. More Bleeders were pouring out as if there were no end to them, their stench overpowering even the smell of blood and bodies littering the ground.

"Well, now we know where they've been all this time," Presley said under his breath. His arms lowered. "We have to fall back."

I glimpsed defeat in his gaze. I narrowed my eyes at the gaping hole in the mountain and started walking forward. I exhaled, releasing the fear holding me captive. As I inhaled, I called on the earth's energy and held my hands out on either side of me. A prickling sensation coursed through my body, and I closed my eyes briefly as it filled me.

I opened my eyes the moment a Bleeder came rushing my way, but Xavier, once more in wolf form, tackled it before it reached me. I kept my eyes on the mountain, my focus unwavering as the hell-spawned creatures got closer. The sound of their feet trampling on the ground and their loud hisses filling the air was enough to drive fear into any warrior. I didn't focus on that, however, or the fact that I stood against an army.

I got down onto one knee and dug my fingers into the earth, sending all the energy I had collected back into it, but aimed at the vampires. Spikes made of earth shot upwards, piercing through the Bleeders' bodies and limbs. I watched as the spikes rolled forward like an ocean wave, impaling and dismembering the Bleeders and Skins, their cries of pain causing the humans and wolves behind me to erupt into cheers.

The feeling of accomplishment, of victory, was short-lived because only a moment passed before more came rushing out of the mountain. "Are you fucking kidding me?" I yelled as I stood up. I spun around to look at Presley.

He paled and raised his guns. "Fall back! Fall back, now!" He started yelling, but then jumped back as black smoke appeared beside him.

Malcolm's face materialized within it. "Am I too late?" Malcolm grinned.

Now, all around us, more demons started to appear. Some looked like normal humans, while others had tails, horns, and wings that dragged behind them. The demons with wings took to the sky and unleashed their power on the vampires. Black crystal-like daggers rained down on the Bleeders and Skins like rain.

Howls rolled up to the sky from within the forest behind us. I closed my eyes and sighed as a feeling of relief washed over me. I turned around to see Axel's wolf, his fur a midnight black against the snow.

Behind him were more wolves than I could count. Among them were other women and men, their cries of anger as loud as the wolves' howling. They kept pouring from the forest, the entire length of the tree line.

This is it. Presley and Xavier appeared at my side. However, my face fell as Axel ran past us along with everyone else. He dove into the Bleeders like a wrecking ball. I swallowed hard, my brows knitted as I felt his rage, his pain.

I placed my hand over my chest as I looked at Xavier's wolf, and he looked at me before rushing forward into the fray.

"Hello, Ruby," a woman said as she appeared by my side. "My name is Ms. Clayton, but you can call me Cassandra."

"Hi. Nice to meet you."

She smiled, her hair a midnight black with a lone streak of white hair that she moved behind her ear. "Axel dated my daughter long ago. Maybe now isn't the time for that story, but I wanted you to know I'm an ally."

My brows touched my hairline as I realized who this woman was.

Axel told me long ago he dated a witch who was killed by a demon possessing a jealous human. This was her mother. "Hi." I shook the hand she held out to me. "Thank you for coming."

She smiled, her eyes a bright violet. She placed her hand on my shoulder. "Axel has told me a lot about you. He is so proud of you, and I am pleased to see how being with you has made him whole again."

"Axel, he seems..." My voice faded away.

She frowned, a pained expression appearing on her face. "We were attacked... half of his pack... his father... they didn't make it." She squeezed my shoulder and walked away as a sword materialized in her hand. She moved expertly among the Bleeders.

I ran forward, my fists clenched. This was our time. The time to teach these creatures what it meant to feel fear.

RUBY

I screamed as a Bleeder turned to ash beneath my hands. I wasn't sure how much time had passed, and I didn't care. All of them—I wanted to kill all of them. The more blood that soaked the snow beneath my feet, the angrier I got, and the more powerful I became.

A foot connected with my side, sending me toppling over. I got back onto my feet quickly, barely feeling the impact. A pulse emitted from my body, sending the Skins, who were rushing towards me, backwards.

I held my hand out and envisioned holding them all by their throats as I pulled them forward once more. Spikes appeared from the earth to impale their bodies. I turned away, moving onto the next Bleeder or Skin I knew had taken the life of an innocent human or supernatural. They had all killed mercilessly, and they would all suffer for it.

Panting, I turned in a circle, taking note of the supernaturals fighting along with us that I'd never seen before. A large black snake shot upward from within the earth, killing two Skins, and I watched as it then turned into a woman. Her forked tongue flicked out of her mouth and she nodded to me before transforming once more and burrowing back into the ground.

I felt it then, a probing within my mind, and I turned around.

Carden backhanded me across my face. I staggered backward, my eyes blurry for a moment, but I caught myself before I fell. When I looked up as my eyes finally cleared, he was already gone.

Suddenly, he appeared in front of me and embedded his sharp nails into my shoulder. I screamed in agony as red-hot pain sped through my body like a bullet train. His red eyes pierced into mine as he quickly pulled his hand out of my shoulder and vanished again when I reached out for him. He appeared once more, his nails piercing into my lower back and thigh at the same time.

Using his vampiric speed, he disappeared yet again, but not before I felt his nail slice down my forearm to my wrist. I fell to my knees as I pressed my right hand to my chest. I couldn't feel my left hand anymore, as if he had damaged the nerve. I could feel the prickling feeling of my body trying to heal itself, but my blood was still oozing from the wound on my arm.

"Accept the Queen's offer, and this ends..." He appeared before me and started walking around me in a circle. "Look around you, Ruby, look at those that are dying. You can stop this with a single action." He came to a stop right in front of me, his uniform stained with blood.

I looked up at him from under my lashes, my leg now going numb, as well.

He went on, "Your power will be equal to our Queen. She has plans for this world, plans that'll be better for everyone if you're on our side. Look at you now—weak and beaten. That will change."

"You know," I gritted out. "I didn't think you'd be the chatty type."

He raised his hand to slap me again, and I fell backward onto the ground.

Just then, a spike appeared from beneath the earth. He stepped back, but not quick enough, and it sliced him across his chest.

"I'll tell you what I told her!" I yelled as it lowered back into the earth, and I pulled myself onto a knee. "I'd rather die than become one of you. I'd rather die than be some kind of pet to you! Freak!" I spat on the ground.

The black veins under his mouth stretched even further up along his face.

I felt him burrowing into my mind, and I groaned as he started to force thoughts and images into my mind. I pressed a finger to my temple, my jaws clenched tightly as I tried to stop seeing the years he'd spent as a vampire. I couldn't push away the images of the decades spent inside the mountain, of the parties and human carnage, of humans being turned as they grew their army for this day.

"Do you think you or anyone here stands a chance against all of us? If you won't come willingly, I'll make you, but I won't fail my Queen!"

"You've already failed her!" I shot back.

He came at me, the intent to kill in his eyes causing them to burn brighter. "Fool!" His nails elongated even further, and he became as pale as I had seen the Queen become.

I tried to stand but couldn't; my leg was still healing.

A wolf appeared out of nowhere and tackled Carden to the ground.

I fell forward as I exhaled with relief when I realized it was Axel in his final form.

The towering black werewolf with the body of a man and beast grabbed Carden by his throat, his nails ripping his flesh.

I looked away as I moved my left shoulder, feeling finally

returning to it as they continued to fight each other while rolling on the ground. Soon they stopped moving.

Axel was over Carden on the ground, their legs tangling together.

I frowned as neither of them moved, but my frown quickly turned to utter gut-wrenching dread as Axel fell off Carden. My hand flew to my chest, Axel's pain hitting my body like a ton of bricks.

Carden removed his arm up to his elbow from Axel's chest.

Axel looked at me, his black eyes fading to hazel as he started to return to his human form, his bones breaking and re-joining.

The sight of the gaping hole in his chest had bile rising to my throat. I fell forward onto my hands, tears instantly springing to my eyes. "No!"

He started gasping for breath, his fingers digging into the earth at his side.

I shook my head, my heartbeat hammering in my head. "No!" I looked at Carden, at the smug grin on his lips, and at Axel's blood dripping from his hand. I fisted my hands on the ground as I released my rage. A shock wave emitted from me, knocking everyone backward, vampire and otherwise. I got to my feet.

Carden's face fell when I moved as quickly as he had been. I appeared before him and grabbed his face. I focused on the black aura around him and began consuming it.

He raised his hand to hit me, the one coated in Axel's blood, but it remained suspended in the air as I used my powers to hold it there. His eyes started to bulge as I pushed him to the ground and climbed onto him. The darkness in him flowed into me, my eyes now black, bottomless pits. I didn't stop as his hunger flowed into me, his memories, and the carnage he'd taken part in. I let it all fuel my rage, my hate, my pain. Soon, he laid beneath me as nothing but a dried-up carcass.

I fell off him, ignoring those that had been watching the entire thing. My focus was on Axel as I crawled to him quickly. My eyes darting over his body frantically as I watched his blood soaking the snow beneath him. "I-it's okay, I-I can heal this." I held my hand over his chest, my eyes burning with tears. I could see inside his body, and he wasn't healing on his own like he should. He started healing, but it stopped. My hand started shaking. "Come on!"

"He punctured my heart, Ruby," he told me, his voice weak. He coughed, blood spluttering from his mouth, dripping down along his chin and neck.

I shook my head as I turned my attention back to his chest. "I can help you! Let me help you, please!"

This can't be happening! Not him, please not him!

My chest was on fire, my insides boiling, as I could feel him slipping away. He closed his eyes, and I screamed his name.

Ms. Clayton ran towards us, her sword falling from her hand.

"Help him! Help him, please!"

"I-I can't—I," she stuttered.

More tears streamed down my cheeks.

"Ruby," Axel called, his sweet voice a mere whisper.

My heart caved. I never told him, I never told him how I felt. We had a rough start, and I held onto it even when he proved to me he deserved my love.

He moved his hand to touch my hair, and as it fell once more, I grabbed it and held it to my chest. "Finish—this..." His Adam's apple bobbed as he swallowed, and his hand slipped out of mine. "I love you." His eyes closed.

My world shattered.

I peered up at Ms. Clayton, who now had tears rolling down her cheeks. I looked around us, at the battle still raging on, at Presley, who had a deep wound running down his leg, but still, he kept reloading his gun. Across the field, my eyes landed on Xavier in his final form. He killed a Skin, ripping its head from its body before turning to me, his large hands folding into fists.

"I love you, too," I whispered to Axel as I called on my power.

Xavier howled as he fell onto all fours and began running towards me.

I called on my power, and the knife the Goddess had given me appeared in my hand. I looked away from Xavier gaining on me. He wouldn't make it in time—he wouldn't stop me. I bent over Axel's body and kissed his already-cold lips, the ache in my chest growing worse.

No one else would die for me, not today.

I plunged the knife into my heart, and the earth around me cracked.

Ms. Clayton, werewolves, demons, and vampires were thrown back roughly, and then pulled forward, only to be thrown again as another wave emitted from my body.

"Thank you," I heard the Goddess say in my mind as my eyes closed. All I could hear was Xavier howling in pain.

When I reopened my eyes, I could feel every living thing around me as if I were directly connected to it all. I looked down at my hands as the black veins there began to crawl up my arm. Soon, my entire body was engulfed in it, even my face. It was as if I were now a passenger in my own body, but I didn't care. I gave everything to the Goddess as I sat in a corner, the feel of Axel's cold lips still on mine.

I touched Axel's body.

He turned to dust and vanished.

As I stood up, thunder rumbled above us. A Bleeder rushed at me, and its thin pale body disintegrated to ash. I turned to face the mountain.

CHAPTER FIFTEEN
PRESLEY

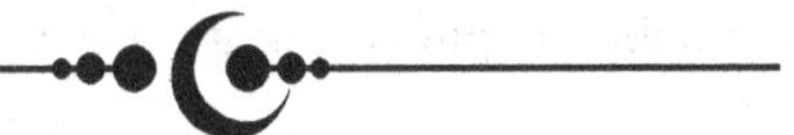

I got to my feet after being knocked over by Ruby's power. I watched as her hair began to change from red to black, the vibrant color changing from the roots downward. Xavier, who was in his wolf form, got up, and when she turned to glance our way, she looked almost unrecognizable.

Her body was covered with black veins. With her midnight-black hair and eyes, she looked every bit of a goddess to me. I knew the person I was looking at was no longer Ruby Saunders. I was stunned with wonder. Right now, the rest of the world literally stood still. No one knew what to expect next. Even the Bleeders had stopped attacking. It appeared they weren't mindless enough to think they'd stand a chance against her.

I was wrong. All at once, as if following some silent command, all the Bleeders went running for her, bypassing us as if we weren't even standing there.

She merely turned to the mountain, and as she waved her hand, the earth beneath us moaned.

I watched as the hole in the mountain cracked further and started breaking, crashing onto the vampires still coming up from within.

She took a step forward, the snow beneath her feet melting. As the Bleeders and Skins got close enough to her, they started bursting into clouds of ash.

Malcolm appeared at my side as Xavier rushed forward, cutting down as many Bleeders and Skins as he could while they focused on attacking Ruby.

She didn't need the help, that was clear. I watched in stunned astonishment as she kept casually walking towards the entrance of the mountain, vampires dying at her feet without her even lifting a hand.

Even I could feel the shift in the atmosphere as heat suddenly surrounded us.

"Shit," Malcolm swore.

I looked in the direction he stared at. He was looking at a demon and a Skin who were battling each other in Ruby's path.

As she drew close, the Skin began to shriek in pain, its skin burning. The demon cried in pain as well, his skin turning red.

Xavier knocked him out of her way.

She kept walking. She didn't even look.

"What the hell," I mumbled under my breath.

Beside me, Malcolm hissed. "That's not Ruby anymore. Anyone in her way will die." He looked around him and placed his finger at his throat. "Stay away from her! Don't get too close! Kill the ones she doesn't!"

"What if she turns on us?" a demon yelled back.

"She won't if you stay the fuck away from her! Let's go!" His voice thundered as if he was using a microphone.

The demons nodded their heads in response.

He ran forward with them but then stopped to look back at me. "Are you coming?"

I looked at the mountain, at the way Ruby had expanded its opening and exhaled. "I'll handle things out here."

I wasn't retreating. The Bleeders around us were few enough for my men and a number of other witches, demons, and werewolves to handle. Fewer and fewer of them were getting by her.

I looked at the blood-soaked ground where Axel's body had been and reloaded my gun.

I turned away, firing five bullets into a Skin before she fell, her body convulsing as the UV bullets burned her from the inside out. Xavier had said if Ruby ever became the Goddess's vessel—she would die.

I glanced over my shoulder at the mountain as Ruby vanished inside. If she didn't die, what would she become?

RUBY

The inside of the mountain didn't look the way I expected it to. It looked as if I had stepped into a hotel that had been raided. I assumed it only looked a mess now because of all the Bleeders and Skins crawling out of a large opening in the ground. I paid no attention to Xavier and the others still locked in battle.

My eyes were on the six guards standing in front of a large elevator. How was there even electricity in here?

"Where is she?" I asked. Inwardly, I frowned because my voice was no longer mine, but that of the Goddess.

The guards in red that we had seen on the video all looked at each other before turning back to me.

I realized they all looked identical. They all had a brown complexion and the same white streak of hair in their black hair.

None of them responded.

I gazed upward. Above me, the ceiling was painted with the same battle we had seen in *The Book of The Damned*, and I wondered if they thought I really needed to use an elevator to get to her. One of them vanished, but I could now track their movements easily, their vampiric speed no longer an issue. The moment he appeared in front of me, his red eyes burning like a flame, my hand darted outward, and the elongated nail on my index finger pierced through his forehead.

His eyes rolled back as black veins appeared from the wound in his forehead, and he fell to the side, his body hitting the ground loudly. It was my turn to act. My lips curved with a smile as I stepped forward and then vanished. I reappeared at the same spot I had been a second later, and a line of blood began to ooze from puncture wounds between all other five vampires.

It felt as if I was doing all of this, and at the same time, I wasn't. I felt the moment my nail pierced their skulls, but my actions were being guided by something else... or someone else, I should say.

"*I need you to give me full control, Ruby. Your conflicted thoughts are restricting me.*" The Goddess's voice echoed in my mind, and without me doing it, my body bounded off the ground towards the ceiling.

"You almost killed a demon out there," I replied as she kept breaking through the ceiling, floor after floor.

"*I don't have time to argue with you, Ruby,*" the Goddess replied impatiently.

Then, within my mind, where I was already partly restricted, I was thrown onto a chair and bound with chains. "Goddess!" I screamed as I tried to break free, but it was futile. She didn't reply. I felt nothing and had no control over anything anymore, and I felt like I was now a bystander in my own body.

All I could do was watch as the Goddess slaughtered every vampire she laid her eyes on before moving onto another floor. I stopped struggling for a moment, my attempts to get free a waste of time. I made the choice to give my body to her, and now I had to live with that choice.

I was here for the time being, but I would die the moment the Goddess left my body. I sighed as she arrived at a room flooded with red lights. At least I'd be able to see Axel, my mother, and Natalie again, but what of Xavier?

I know I'd broken his heart; I had felt it.

Countless humans were cowering in the corners, either naked or barely clothed, some wearing nothing but collars around their necks.

The Goddess only glanced at them before walking towards the door at the end of the hall.

The moment she got close enough, it was thrown open, and Amythia walked out, her wings emerging from her back. She smiled widely. Her fangs descended as her face began to morph into something hideous, and her skin turned an ugly shade of grey. Her eyes grew large as her ears became long and pointy. "You're foolish to stand against me, Ruby," she smirked. "I gave you the chance to willingly join me. Now that option is no longer available to you."

The Goddess shook her head. "Is that so?" The Goddess replied as they began walking in a circle. "Can you repeat what that offer was? I'm afraid I'm not Ruby."

Amythia stopped walking as she narrowed her eyes. "Yes, you're right. You're the Goddess bitch now, aren't you?"

The Goddess's lips parted to speak—*my* lips parted.

Then without warning, Amythia charged at us—at the Goddess—ice dagger in hand. The Goddess moved quickly, appearing beside Amythia and grabbing her by one of her wings. She released Amythia swiftly as Amythia's other wing bent at an odd angle, the claw-like spike at the tip of her wing missing The Goddess's face by an inch.

I winced as I watched. After all, this body was still mine for now. If the Goddess lost a hand or a finger, it was my body being dismembered, not hers.

Both women fought viciously, the Goddess taking blow after blow while delivering some of her own. I tried to escape from the chains, but each time I tried—they grew tighter. I gave up as the

Goddess threw Amythia into the wall, the impact causing the wall to shatter as Amythia fell through.

She got to her feet, her already-deformed face twisted with fury that one of her wings was broken. She exhaled, and fog drifted from her mouth as frost began to crawl up the walls. As quickly as it formed, it began to melt, a clash of fire and ice within the room.

To my surprise, Amythia reached behind her and ripped her broken wing from her back. "I bet when you talked to Ruby, you failed to mention that the Goddess who was raped by the Demon King and gave birth to my kind was your sister."

"That's not information any mortal needs to know," the Goddess retorted.

My eyes widened in shock.

"I think they'd find it interesting to know that you are only helping in this fight because of your own need for vengeance, your obsession with eradicating my kind," Amythia replied silkily, and she stepped back as the heat coming from the Goddess grew intense. She smiled.

I found it odd that the Goddess didn't seem to realize Amythia was only taunting her. While Amythia's revelation was surprising to me, it explained a lot. I didn't see any other deities intervening the way the Goddess had.

"Make no mistake, Amythia, this is where your bloodline ends. You don't have any offspring, and your Generals are dead. You have no one to pass your power or throne to. When you die, the creatures you have plaguing this world will die, too." The Goddess laughed mockingly. "You're not welcome in the demon realm, and nor that of the Gods. You're nothing, and you'll die as the queen of nothing."

Amythia's crimson eyes seemed to burn even brighter as the Goddess's laughter and harsh words appeared to have their intended effect. "We'll see who dies today!"

Both women ran forward, their bodies colliding in a clash of power and years of built-up animosity.

Behind them, Xavier rushed into the room in his human form, along with Malcolm and a few others. They ran forward, but even with the Goddess's cry that they shouldn't... it was too late.

Ice daggers shot towards them from Amythia's back.

The Goddess held her hand out, a flame burst from her fingers to melt the daggers, but not before some of the daggers had met their targets.

Amythia backhanded the Goddess across her face and then sank her fangs into the Goddess' arm.

The chains around me loosened, and I quickly unbound myself as the Goddess grabbed Amythia's face with her other hand. Steam began to rise from beneath the Goddess's hand.

Amythia released the Goddess' arm, tearing the flesh. Two wolves bravely tackled her, but she killed them with ease. One of her eyes was burned shut and swollen, but she smiled widely before bursting into laughter.

For a moment, I could feel what the Goddess was feeling again as she looked down at her arm—*my* arm—with the flesh hanging loosely. I could feel the Queen's venom making its way up my arm.

To my surprise, the Goddess raised her other hand and sliced the arm off.

Amythia's face fell.

The Goddess smiled haughtily. "Did you think turning me would be that easy?"

Pain wracked me as my body started to break, and I wished I hadn't gotten up from that chair. The Goddess started to shift into a wolf, and I felt the entire transformation. My body was torn apart, only to be mended back together into a brand new form. Soon, a large white wolf stood where the Goddess had been. She growled threateningly at Amythia.

I laid on the ground in my mind as the Goddess continued to do what she wished with my body. I was awash with cold sweat, my eyes wide at the traumatizing pain I had just felt. I hadn't been ready for it.

"Ruby?" The Goddess called to me.

I looked up weakly.

"I'm sorry, my child," she said apologetically as she bent down to move my hair from my face. "I'm sorry for this pain, but I'm proud of you. We don't have much time left. Your body can't take much more of this."

I started crying because I'd truly had enough. The life I was given wasn't mine, and because of that, I'd suffered my entire life. There were moments that were good, but how many of those moments were good compared to the ones that were bad?

"I hate you for making him mine, and then taking him from me!" I started crying. "Axel... Axel died saving me because of you!"

She sighed, then cocked her head to something behind me. "You'll be free of this suffering soon. You'll be able to join them."

I looked over my shoulder.

My mother, Axel, and Natalie stood there. They looked like they were glowing, their smiles wide as they waved at me.

I sat up as I wiped at my tears, my heart filling with joy from seeing them, but I shook my head. "I can't leave Xavier." I turned back around to face her. "Please, I can't do this to him. I just—I used the knife—I just wanted this to end, but I can't leave him to suffer from losing his mate. The pain might kill him. I would have killed him!"

"The pain might make him stronger," the Goddess replied as she stood up. She pointed behind me.

I looked around.

Axel was directly behind me in his wolf form. His eyes were hazel instead of black.

"Go to him, Ruby," the Goddess advised calmly. "I want you to trust me, okay? Trust me, I won't let this be the way your life ends."

I reached out, and as I plunged my paws into Axel's black fur, a feeling of being at home took over. The Goddess vanished, and I was once again cut off from her emotions and feelings.

Back inside the room, Amythia's other wing was broken. The Goddess was limping due to a deep gash down one of her front legs, and Xavier was now lying on the floor with an ice dagger in his thigh and shoulder. The bodies of other demons and werewolves littered the ground around them.

Although there was blood running down his face and he looked a little worse for wear, Malcolm was still standing.

The Goddess's hind legs suddenly snapped backward.

Amythia's eyes widened with fear. She rushed forward but was swiftly engulfed by Malcolm's black smoke.

He gritted his teeth as he tried to hold her as the Goddess shifted into her final form.

I smiled. Even though it wasn't truly me, I felt proud at the majestic creature my body became. The Goddess's white wolf, now on two legs, howled so loud the earth trembled.

Amythia broke free of Malcolm's hold, but as she tried to attack him, the Goddess attacked her. She grabbed Amythia's face and hand. Before Amythia had a second to counter-attack, the Goddess' wolf bit down hard on Amythia's neck, piercing skin and flesh to the bone.

The Goddess shook her like a rag doll.

Malcolm hurried to help Xavier up before pulling the daggers from his body.

"We can't leave Ruby," Xavier told Malcolm.

I looked over at Axel by my side as tears began to stream down my face.

Black veins began to appear on The Goddess's body, and it slowly started to enter Amythia, who was stabbing the Goddess with her nails, trying and failing to break free from her hold.

"Ruby is at peace. Leave!" The Goddess shouted.

I knew she was speaking into the minds of Xavier and Malcolm.

"Now!" she yelled insistently.

Xavier started to protest. I looked away as it took the four remaining werewolves and Malcolm to drag him from the room.

The mountain began to moan, almost as if it were in pain, as pieces of the ceiling began to fall around us.

It started to burn where the Goddess had bitten Amythia's body, and she became covered with black veins. Her pale skin started turning red and bubbling. It was like she was being burned from the inside out.

The Goddess simply ignored the numerous cuts and wounds Amythia's claws inflicted as she fought for her life. It was clear at this point that Amythia's fighting was futile.

I could hear the shrieks and cries of the other vampires as they sensed their Queen dying and felt her pain.

"I want to speak to him! Please, Goddess, let me say goodbye!"

"Speak!" she yelled back.

I closed my eyes as I envisioned Xavier's face. I thought back to the first moment I saw him so long ago in that library. I re-lived our first kiss.

"I love you so much!" I choked out, and I heard his cries of pain in my mind in response.

The Goddess crushed Amythia's body to her as they—we— exploded, taking the mountain along with us.

• • •

XAVIER

I could feel her dying.

As I was dragged from the room, my cries and protests were ignored as I felt Ruby slipping away. As she went—my heart broke piece by piece.

Amythia was destroying her body, ripping into her flesh to break free, but still, Ruby held onto her.

She promised me—swore to me—she wouldn't do this!

I was dragged outside and held by my own men to stop me from rushing back inside as the mountain began to crumble. All around us, vampires were withering on the ground in pain, their bodies burning. All I could focus on was Ruby leaving me. As she had grown stronger, so did our bond. She could feel me, and she could feel Axel, the way it was for pureblood wolves. I felt like our bond was finally complete, and now she was leaving me!

I stopped fighting, my body going numb as I heard her voice echo in my mind.

"I love you so much."

"No! No! Ruby!"

The mountain exploded, knocking everyone close backward with debris flying everywhere.

A large rock knocked me over, and I groaned as I moved it off of me. As the dust started to clear, I stared at the mountain. The last piece of my heart, the piece that had held on after hearing Ruby's voice, broke into tiny pieces and disintegrated.

I could no longer feel her. In the spot where she had been, I felt hollow, as if my heart had been carved out of my body and removed.

Half of the mountain was destroyed. I fell forward, my fists beating the ground until my hands were bloody. My fangs and nails elongated. Hot tears streamed down my face, and I didn't care if I wasn't upholding the werewolf way of not showing emotion.

I placed my hands on my head.

Malcolm fell to his knees beside me, his face slick with tears.

I howled to the clearing sky above us until I lost my voice, and a dead silence settled around us.

For others, the war had been won, but for me—I'd lost everything.

CHAPTER SIXTEEN
XAVIER

SIX MONTHS LATER

"*It's been six months since the vampire invasion turned the world upside down. Cities are being rebuilt, but for many citizens of the world, life will never be the same. A bill to outlaw the killing of werewolves and all other supernatural creatures has finally been approved after months of debate. However, many humans are still scared and skeptical of the supernaturals walking among them.*"

I switched the TV off and reclined in my chair. Still, the black market sales of captured supernaturals wasn't being reported in the news. I understood the fear the humans felt of the unknown right outside their door, of the beings more powerful than them. When they looked at us, they didn't see us as individuals capable of both good and bad. They grouped us all together and decided we should be feared. Supernaturals were capable of feeling fear, as well. We were still being hunted and exploited for our powers and abilities.

I looked down at the numerous files on my desk. Werewolves were once more falling into the protector role, just as we had so long ago. With Presley's help, a task force of supernaturals and humans had been created to keep the world in balance, or attempt to, as we all tried to adjust to this new normal.

I looked at Ruby's picture on my desk and swallowed as an ache rippled within my chest. The pain of losing her hadn't faded. The loss was still raw after so many months. I knew it would remain that way until the moment I saw her again on the other side. Thankfully, assuming the role of the new Alpha of the Blackmoon pack kept me busy and helped me to remain grounded enough not to lose myself in the grief. Yet, on nights like this, the pain of not having her by my side as Luna was almost unbearable.

Leaving my office, I made my way outside, where torches were erected as we feasted under a new full moon.

Randoll patted me on the shoulder as he walked by me, his arm over his mate's shoulder.

I watched them with a smile as they gazed at each other with love.

"Alpha Xavier," a small voice called from behind me.

I turned around to see little Accalia running towards me. I bent down to her level, and she ran into my arms.

I faked falling over from the force. "How many times have I told you not to run around like that, miss? I would hate to see you fall and hurt yourself, but most of all, hurt someone else. Don't you know how strong you are?"

Her smile widened. "I fell yesterday, and I didn't cry. Mommy says I'm going to be the strongest one in the pack when I grow up." She moved her black, curly hair from her eyes.

I nodded. "Your mom is right. Do you know why you'll be the strongest?"

She nodded.

"Why?" I asked.

She glanced at her mother, who was watching us. "Because I'm an Enchanted," she grinned as she looked at me, her brown doe eyes bright with pride.

"That's right. You're special. There was a girl in our pack that was special, just like you. Did you know that? Two of them, actually."

She bobbed her head vigorously. "Natalie and Ruby!" she exclaimed enthusiastically, catching the attention of a few other wolves nearby.

"That's right. Natalie and Ruby were Enchanteds just like you, and two of the most powerful." I poked her chin and her giggle washed away some of the sadness that had settled on my heart. "You will follow in their footsteps and be the third most powerful. Okay?"

"Why did they have to die?" she suddenly asked.

My brows knitted. My arms twitched as my wolf awoke at the mention of their deaths.

Her mother quickly took her from me.

I clenched my fists, knowing my eyes had changed to black. "Forgive me." I looked away before glancing back at her, ashamed as Accalia looked at me with uncertainty.

Her mother smiled sadly at me. "There is no need for that," she told me and ushered Accalia away.

I stood there for a moment as I closed my eyes to focus on my breathing, to focus on the sounds and smells around me. I needed to ground myself to avoid getting lost in my grief.

"Are you okay?" my father asked with concern.

I nodded without turning to face him. After a moment, I opened my eyes and exhaled through my mouth, my racing heartbeat slowing. "I'm fine," I told him as I turned around. "I'm getting better at controlling the bursts of anger." Laughter met my ears, and we both looked Randoll's way as he and his mate and a few other wolves chatted among themselves. "The loneliness is what's most painful."

"I wish I could say you'll get used to it, but you never really will. At least, I haven't," he said sadly.

I looked his way.

"You'll always feel like half of your soul is gone, but it'll get easier to work around as the years go by. You'll find new ways to cope with it."

Right now, it felt like that might never happen.

"Presley's team found werewolf remains in a warehouse yesterday." Since he'd stepped down as Alpha but still needed to keep himself busy, he'd joined the P.I.A., the Paranormal Investigation Agency. Now he worked with General Presley. "The whole thing is being covered up, though."

"We sacrificed everything to save the world, but as we expected, the humans are being humans."

"Yes, but I mean we got orders to cover it up," he clarified.

I pulled a face, my interest piqued.

He nodded. "We found out the warehouse was purchased a few months back by a shell company."

His words rolled around in my mind. "Again, I'm not surprised. I knew it would only be a matter of time before someone decided to round us up and turn us into test subjects, with or without our consent." I shook my head as I looked away, my eyes moving from one wolf to the next, and my fists clenched. "I understand the hatred Axel had for them."

Dad didn't respond, but from my peripheral vision, I could see he was studying me closely. "Not all of them are bad, Xavier. Please remember that. She was one of them."

"She was never one of them!" I bit back.

Above us, a clap of thunder echoed through the night, followed by lightning.

Two bolts struck the ground, and the night returned to silence.

Dad looked me up and down strangely.

I shook my head. "That wasn't me."

"Well, that can't be anything good," he replied.

Suddenly, an echo of gasps erupted through the pack.

Dad and I walked forward as a crowd started to form. My Alpha instincts kicked in and had me walking forward quickly, ready to defend my home and my people. However, I didn't make it very far before I froze in my tracks.

A scent I didn't think I'd ever smell again washed over me.

Beside me, my dad gasped, "This isn't possible."

I rushed forward in an instant, and the crowd parted for me, my anxiety rising. As I came to a stop in front of the crowd, I watched as everyone else stood with their mouths open in shock as two wolves walked from out of the darkness of the forest.

My heart grew heavy as I stared at the black and white wolves. I reached up and combed my hair back with both hands, praying to the Goddess my eyes weren't playing tricks on me.

There stood Axel and Ruby.

A short laugh of bewilderment escaped my lips. "Ruby?" I asked in disbelief.

The white wolf walked forward, her head low as she smelled the ground, but her eyes were on me.

"Is it really you, Ruby?" I stared into her black eyes, and I got my answer as they began to change to the stunning emerald eyes that had haunted my dreams for months.

She whimpered as her shoulder dislocated.

Both of them began to shift, fur turning to skin and paws turning into hands and feet.

Laying on the ground, naked, was Axel and Ruby.

Axel rose quickly, brushing the dirt and leaves off.

Ruby remained lying on her side, her knees pulled up to her chest.

I quickly took my jacket off and covered her, my eyes roaming her face. I reached out, my hand shaking as I moved her red hair from her face.

"Xavier?" she whispered.

I felt as if my heart would explode with joy. I picked her up slowly and crushed her to my body. I kept taking deep breaths, inhaling as much of her scent as I could just in case she suddenly vanished. "How?" I asked as I placed her gently onto her feet.

My dad joined us to give Axel pants.

"How is this even possible? You died." I looked at Axel as he pulled his zipper up, his curly hair now down his back. "You both died."

"The Goddess sent us back," Ruby responded softly.

Behind us, whispers erupted among the pack.

"I-I don't remember what happened after I died," she went on to explain. "I just woke up in the forest, but..." she placed her hand over her heart as she frowned. Her eyes became teary. "I do know that's the last time I'll ever shift." Her hand fell away from her chest as she smiled sadly. "I'm only a half-breed now."

I stepped closer to her and shook my head as I took her hand into mine. I couldn't believe I was touching her, seeing her, hearing her. "You've never *only* been half anything, Ruby. You're so much more than just a half-breed. You're the woman who gave her life to save us all. You're our pack's Luna, and most importantly, you're my whole world." I wiped away a tear that escaped her eye. "You're home now."

Turning to Axel, I exhaled heavily. "You gave your life to save her. For that and more, you're welcome to join our pack. I'm sorry about your father and the wolves you lost. The ones that survived are already among our ranks."

He nodded as he looked around us, a smile growing on his lips. "Thanks, Xavier, and thank you for keeping my pack members safe when I was gone. As for myself, like Ruby, I don't remember where we were or what happened after I died, but I do remember there are plans I need to see through."

"Okay," I said.

Suddenly, we were bombarded by pack members who greeted Axel, and then Ruby was dragged away from us. Questions of how she was alive and where she'd been were thrown at her from all directions.

"I'm still mated to her," Axel told me.

I took a deep intake of breath. "Yeah, I figured," I muttered low.

"How are we going to do this, then?" He tilted his head to the side to look at me. "Neither of us is going to reject her."

"The world has changed, Axel. I doubt anyone will care anymore if she's mated to the two of us." I watched her as her voice drifted to me on the cool night's wind while she clutched at the front of my jacket to cover herself up.

Spending months without her had been the worst time of my life. I had prayed to the Goddess to send her back to me, and she had answered. I had begged night after night for this. I swore to the Goddess I'd be fine with her being mated to Axel as long as I got to be with her again, as long as I got to see her smile. Our relationship might be taboo, but her loving him didn't mean she loved me any less, or vice versa. "We both love her. We'd both die for her, and I think that's enough common ground for us. That's all that's needed to make this work."

He watched her as well, his arms crossing over his chest. Along with the longer hair, he looked considerably more muscular than when he had died.

Ruby looked a little different too. She had a glow to her skin that hadn't been there before. They must've been with the gods for a while.

What had it been like? What happened to them? "Can you tell me if you guys saw Natalie?" I inquired hopefully.

Axel sighed. "No, I can't remember anything. I think that's maybe for the best."

I nodded.

He uncrossed his arms as he turned to face me.

My eyes drifted to him, curious as to why he was watching me so intently.

"But I don't doubt that she's happy. Something in me tells me Ruby and I were too. Tell me, Xavier, are you sure this is something we can do, this relationship, while you two lead this pack?"

"Do you love her?" I asked him.

He frowned. "Yes, of course I do. She's my whole world—my everything."

I nodded as I held my hand out to him.

He hesitated only briefly before shaking my hand.

An unspoken truce formed between us.

"And you'll always be a part of this pack, whether you live here with us or not." I nodded at him. "So as far as I can see, that's all we need to make this work."

◦•◦ ◦•◦

AXEL
TWO YEARS LATER

I leaned against the window as I stared up at the full moon hanging low in the sky.

Behind me, Xavier kept pacing back and forth.

I closed my eyes as I finally had enough. "Would you stop doing that? You're not helping my anxiety," I growled.

He stopped pacing. "Anxiety? You look perfectly calm to me," he shot back in a loud tone.

I turned to face him. I shrugged my jacket off and sighed as I threw it over the back of a chair. I then removed my tie and unbuttoned my shirt. I had flown 16 hours straight to get here. I was dying for a bath and something to eat, but none of that was more important than what was currently happening. "I'm not calm at all. When I took Olcan's place as Council member, I had to master the art of appearing impassive to everything. Apparently, it's starting to become second nature." I sighed. "How's the pack been?"

Xavier sat down, his leg tapping the ground nervously, then he made a face. "Really? You want to talk about the pack right now?"

I shrugged as I turned back to the window. "Just making conversation. It's better than panicking."

"Are they here yet?" Malcolm inquired impatiently as he entered the room.

I looked over my shoulder to see him carrying a black stuffed bear that was almost as big as he was. "What the hell is that?" I asked with a chuckle.

He placed the hideous thing down on a chair. "It's a teddy bear. What does it look like?" He patted its large head. "It's for my grandkids. I'm going to be a granddad now."

"Yes, we know. You tell that to literally everyone who will listen to you," Mathieu chimed in with a laugh as he sat down, the wooden chair squeaking under his weight. "So, how is she?"

"Still in labor," Xavier groaned with an exhausted sigh, as if he were the one in labor. "We can't even hear what's going on in there. Turning the office into our bedroom was a bad idea."

"Ruby wanted privacy." I shrugged. The office had those special sound-proof walls, which had seemed ideal for a bedroom in a house full of werewolves, but right now, I just wanted to know what the hell was going on in there.

Xavier snorted.

Mathieu chuckled. "I was like this when your mother went into labor, but of course, she wasn't like Ruby. We've never had a half-human, half-Enchanted give birth in our pack."

"Well, there is a first time for everything," Malcolm added, his green eyes—so like his daughter's—bright with excitement.

It was nice to see him looking so cheerful. I know how important it was to Ruby that the deal he had made with that demon was broken. It had taken some time, but it had finally happened. With the two years that passed, the war that took my life and Ruby's already seemed like a lifetime ago.

The world had transformed as supernaturals grew more

accepted day by day. There were those who still remained hidden because there were humans that still preyed upon and exploited them. Yet, for the most part, a new dawn had begun.

The pack nurse walked in, blood smeared on her scrubs.

Xavier jumped to his feet.

I stepped forward. "Where is she?" I questioned, my words coming out more forceful than I intended.

"Are the babies okay?" Xavier added.

She smiled at us, amused at our obviously panicked state.

I didn't find it amusing at all.

After one of the babies turned the wrong way, Xavier and I had been pushed from the room and locked out. The pack nurse was on my shit list for that one.

"She's fine, and the babies are healthy. You can see them now." The nurse stepped to the side.

Xavier rushed by her, a quick thanks leaving his lips.

"Thank you," I told her as I rushed from the room as well, hot on Xavier's heels.

I was right behind him as he opened the door. My eyes immediately landed on the love of our lives with our kids in her arms. She looked at us standing at the door, and the nervousness I had been feeling for hours faded away.

She smiled at us.

As if commanded, we both moved forward at the same time.

In her arms were both babies. One was wrapped in a pink blanket while the other was swaddled in blue.

We stood on either side of her.

I leaned down and kissed her forehead.

Xavier did the same.

Malcolm and Mathieu finally joined us, Malcolm carrying in his massive teddy bear.

I became completely focused on the tiny little bundles of love in Ruby's arms.

She looked exhausted, her hair damp and knotted, with her eyes puffy from crying.

"You did great, babe." I ran a finger down her cheek.

"We're so proud of you," Xavier added.

She closed her eyes for a moment as she smiled and laid her head back against her pillow. "I'm so tired," she said weakly. "Let's not do this again."

We all chuckled.

The nurse joined us to do some final checks on Ruby.

I took the time to admire my kids—our kids—as the nurse checked them out as well.

The girl—our daughter—had red curly hair, my hazel eyes and Xavier's full lips, while our son had Xavier's dark hair, Ruby's emerald eyes, and my brown complexion. Both kids were the perfect blend of Xavier, Ruby, and me.

A feeling of accomplishment I'd never felt before filled me. The amount of love I already had within me for these kids felt overwhelming and scary.

"You guys can hold them, you know. You don't have to stand there staring like that," Ruby told us softly.

Xavier paled.

I reached down and took the little girl from her, my heart swelling so much it felt like it would explode within me.

After a moment, Xavier reached down and took the boy into his arms.

We both looked at each other, a message that *this is real, we're fathers* passing between us.

It was as if in a matter of hours, the world had changed. It would never be the same for us again.

"Have you all decided on names?" Malcolm stepped forward.

"The girl will be named Natalie," Ruby announced, her eyes becoming a little teary.

"Perfect," Xavier mumbled as he began to bounce somewhat.

"And we decided on Caleb for the boy," he added as he looked to me for confirmation.

"After weeks of fighting about it," I shot back.

He rolled his eyes.

Sometimes I could not figure out how Ruby managed to put up with this man on a regular basis.

She was incredibly stubborn, though—even worse than me.

Xavier and I had come a long way from where we started, when I had wanted to rip his throat out each time I saw him close to Ruby. Now we shared a three-way mating bond, a pack, and two babies with her.

Being a Council member meant being away from the pack for long periods, but knowing Xavier was here with her made it easier for me. I knew he was the only other person that would do whatever it took to protect her. Taking on the responsibility I had meant I'd been able to make sure werewolves finally had the rights and freedom they deserved. Yet I never would've been able to do that if I didn't have Xavier at home protecting all that was important to me in this life.

It pained me sometimes to be away from my family and my pack, but now, looking down at this precious little girl in my arms, I knew I would do anything to make sure she and her brother grew up in a world that was safe for them.

———— ••● ●•• ————

Ruby

"Okay, that's enough, we want to hold our grandkids." Mathieu reached out and took his grandson from Xavier.

Malcolm took Natalie from Axel.

They all looked so happy as they bickered among themselves about who would be teaching which of the kids what. I didn't want to tell them all I was dying to rest.

My body felt broken, and I felt like I was staying awake from sheer will to see the guys with the kids. The complications started when we discovered Caleb had turned the wrong way during my labor. Thankfully, the nurse was able to coax the breech baby into the right position, but there was no time to call the guys back into the room before the twins were born. Babies have a mind of their own sometimes, and these two just couldn't wait to join the world. They might have inherited a hint of Xavier's impatience as well.

"Oh, no," I interjected as I wagged my finger at Axel. "My daughter will not be groomed to become a Council member, and Caleb will make his own choices, Xavier. My kids will have control over their own lives, over their own destiny, so kindly do not make plans for them. They're only a few hours old, after all."

"Well, the Luna has spoken." Xavier chuckled as he winked at me.

Axel started laughing. "Suckup," he mumbled under his breath.

"Prick," Xavier shot back.

I pressed a finger to my temple. Caleb and Natalie weren't the only kids I had to deal with around here, and it showed. "Can you both please stop it?" I groaned.

Axel sat down beside my bed. "How are you feeling?" he asked.

I looked over at Xavier, Mathieu, and Malcolm as they continued to gush over the babies. "Like I finally have the family I always wanted," I told him.

He picked up my hand and kissed the back of it. "How do they both have features from all three of us? I don't think that's normal."

I shrugged at his question, as I had no idea. That had been my first thought when I saw them, but given how our story had gone so far, why should anything surprise me? "Normal isn't a word that should be in our vocabulary at this point. I'm a human and Enchanted, I was also a deity for a short time, and I'm mated to two werewolves. Normal doesn't exist for us."

He nodded in agreement before rolling the sleeves of his shirt up to reveal his muscular arms, covered heavily in tattoos.

"I've missed you." I pouted. The way he smiled back at me made me feel like all he saw was the most beautiful woman in the world, no matter how I looked after pushing out two babies. "Will you be able to stay a while before going back to Albania?"

"They'll have to drag me away kicking and screaming because I'm not planning on leaving here for a while," he answered.

Xavier suddenly turned to us. "What? You're staying?"

Axel grinned at him.

Xavier's face twisted with a little disappointment in response.

I closed my eyes as they started to bicker again, but it was cut short as Natalie made a sound and once more had their attention.

I smiled, as it reminded me of how Natalie had been. She knew how to gain the attention of everyone in an instant. I sighed as I remembered her gorgeous blue eyes. I hoped she would watch over my kids from the gods' realm.

My chest tightened because more than anything, I wished she was here with us. I gasped and pulled my hand up to my chest as a chill ran down my arms.

The guys turned to me, concern written on their faces.

"Are you okay, Ruby?" Malcolm moved forward.

I held my hand up and nodded. "I'm okay, I'm just tired."

He nodded. "You should get some rest."

I turned my head to the side to stare out the window across the room as the chill that had run down my arm traveled down my cheek as well. I bit my lip to hold back my tears because I knew, deep within me, it was Natalie. "Hey, old friend," I muttered under my breath as my eyes grew heavy, my lids lowering a little. As the moon's light shone through the window, I swore I saw a brief glimpse of glowing blonde hair and bright blue eyes peeking in.

I recalled a conversation I had with her so long ago. She jokingly said she might never have kids, but she promised I'd get the family I deserved, and that would be her family, too. Back then,

I hadn't thought much of it. Yet she had known so much, she might have known this was how everything would end. I could not imagine carrying the burden of being aware of your own death, yet continuing on with life with a positive outlook, as if there would be no end. Natalie was my hero, a daily inspiration to trust and accept my fate while living life to its fullest.

I hoped my daughter grew up to be as brave and strong as Natalie was.

"Guess what," I whispered as my eyes finally closed. "I finally have the family you promised. I finally have *our* family."

LUNA RISING WORLD

Want to know what happened before Luna Rising?
Read Bloodmoon Wars Series!

BLOODMOON WARS SERIES

The Awakening

The Enlightenment

The Revolution

The Renaissance

The New Age

Ever wonder what happens after a wolf dies?
Read Wolf Reborn series to find out!

THE WOLF REBORN SERIES

Wolf Reborn

Wolf Burdened

Wolf Scorned

Wolf Fallen

Wolf Embraced

OTHER SERIES BY SARA SNOW

DESTINE ACADEMY

Destine Academy - The Complete Series

CURSED MATES SERIES

Cursed Mates

Cursed Pack

Cursed Storm

Cursed Rage

Cursed Fates

GEMINI WOLVES

Moon Pledged

Moon Touched

Moon Promised

SHATTERED KINGDOM

Shattered Kingdom

Stolen Kingdom

Ruined Kingdom

VENANDI CHRONICLES

Demon Marked

Demon Kissed

Demon Huntress

Demon Desire

Demon Eternal

THE FALLEN BLOOD SERIES

Dark Mate

Fallen Mate

Runaway Mate

Replaced Mate

Broken Mate

Eternal Mate

www.ingramcontent.com/pod-product-compliance
Lightning Source LLC
Chambersburg PA
CBHW010845190726
48286CB00012BA/3000